"I was flattered when I heard how you felt about me...

"Even though your feelings might be misguided."

She frowned. "You were flattered? Then why did you avoid me?"

Jonathan shrugged. "Because I didn't know what to say. I'm really not all that great."

Natalie burst out laughing and suddenly the ice was broken between them. "Thanks for that," she laughed. "I think I've been taking this way too seriously. I guess we could both learn to lighten up."

"Yeah, we could."

Natalie looked up and found Jonathan looking at her in a way she'd never seen before. They stared at each other for several long, compelling seconds. It set her pulse racing and Natalie had to remind herself that Jonathan wasn't interested in her. She was a curvy woman with a couple extra inches around her middle so there was no way he was interested in her. Yet...there was something dangerous in his stare.

* * *

Vacation Crush
by Yahrah St. John is part of the
Texas Cattleman's Club: Ranchers and Rivals series.

Dear Reader,

I was excited to be asked to be a part of Harlequin Desire's long-running Texas Cattleman's series. *Vacation Crush* is book five in the Ranchers and Rivals miniseries. There are a lot of secrets and mysteries to solve, but romance is at the center.

My characters Jonathan Lattimore and Natalie Hastings didn't have a meet-cute, but their story has an unforgettable start when Natalie accidentally goes live in front of the entire town and confesses her feelings for Jonathan. My favorite part of writing the book was watching Jonathan's progression from a gun-shy cowboy with a fear of commitment to a man ready for love.

Alternately, the adage that dreams do come true happens for Natalie because the longtime crush she had on Jonathan turns into something more when sparks fly at a beachside resort in Galveston. Natalie goes after what she wants and when push comes to shove, she won't settle for less than the love she deserves. Hope you enjoy this sensual and sexy summer read.

Want more YSJ news? Sign up for my newsletter at www.yahrahstjohn.com or write me at yahrah@yahrahstjohn.com.

Yours truly,

Yahrah St. John

YAHRAH ST. JOHN

VACATION CRUSH

HARLEQUIN
DESIRE

Special thanks and acknowledgment are given to Yahrah St. John for her contribution to the Texas Cattleman's Club: Ranchers and Rivals miniseries.

HARLEQUIN®
DESIRE™

Recycling programs for this product may not exist in your area.

ISBN-13: 978-1-335-58132-7

Vacation Crush

Copyright © 2022 by Harlequin Enterprises ULC

For questions and comments about the quality of this book, please contact us at CustomerService@Harlequin.com.

Harlequin Enterprises ULC
22 Adelaide St. West, 41st Floor
Toronto, Ontario M5H 4E3, Canada
www.Harlequin.com

Printed in U.S.A.

Yahrah St. John became a writer at the age of twelve when she wrote her first novella after secretly reading a Harlequin romance. She's the proud author of forty-three books with Kimani Romance and Harlequin Desire plus her own indie books.

When she's not at home crafting one of her steamy romances with compelling heroes and feisty heroines with a dash of family drama, she is gourmet cooking or traveling the globe seeking out her next adventure. For more info: www.yahrahstjohn.com.

Books by Yahrah St. John

Harlequin Desire

The Stewart Heirs

At the CEO's Pleasure
His Marriage Demand
Red Carpet Redemption

Locketts of Tuxedo Park

Consequences of Passion
Blind Date with the Spare Heir
Holiday Playbook
A Game Between Friends

Texas Cattleman's Club

Vacation Crush

Visit her Author Profile page at Harlequin.com, or yahrahstjohn.com, for more titles.

You can also find Yahrah St. John on Facebook, along with other Harlequin Desire authors, at Facebook.com/harlequindesireauthors!

To my friend Kiara Ashanti,
who pushes me to keep writing
even when I hit a wall.

One

Never let 'em see you sweat. That's what Natalie Hastings reminded herself when she walked into the Royal Diner and all eyes trained on her. She kept her head high, letting her jet-black microbraids swing in the wind as she sat down in a booth in the corner of the diner. Natalie had maintained a low profile since the infamous Texas Cattleman's summer bash last month. She had made a horrible fool of herself in front of the entire club by confessing her secret crush on Jonathan Lattimore to her best friend, Chelsea Grandin, while on Facebook Live.

Her feelings for the sexy rancher had been on display for the entire crowd. She had no idea they had switched from the prerecorded videos to going live. Luckily, only her voice was heard on the jumbotron as she talked to Chelsea while Aubrey Collins set up Facebook Live. But to make matters worse, she was certain Jonathan had heard every word. Once she came from the filming tent, she'd been stunned to see everyone pointing and snickering at her. Her grandmother Claudette Hastings pulled her aside and to her horror filled Natalie in on the details. She wanted to talk to Jonathan and explain, but he was nowhere to be found. And since then, he had actively avoided her. Although they weren't close, they did run in the same social circles. She was hurt that Jonathan wouldn't at least talk to her. If nothing else, she thought they were friends, but it sure didn't feel that way now.

When is this going to blow over? Natalie thought. Wasn't there some other gossip the citizens of Royal could talk about? Like Chelsea getting engaged to Nolan Thurston, the hunky twin of Heath Thurston who was making a claim against Chelsea's family's ranch. No...instead, they were gossiping about why Natalie was crushing on a man who never paid her one ounce of attention.

"Natalie, so great to see you," Gloria Brown, the diner's waitress, said when she came to her table. "Where have you been hiding yourself, darling?"

"Hiding?" Natalie played dumb but Gloria knew how much she loved the diner's peach pie. She treated herself to the delicious confection at least once a month.

The older woman smiled and patted her shoulder. "Don't go being a stranger because some tongues in this town are wagging. You have nothing to be ashamed of. That Lattimore boy would make a fine match for any woman, especially a woman as smart as you."

"Mrs. Brown," Natalie whispered to make sure no one else heard her. "Can we please change the subject?"

"Sure thing. What can I get you?"

"I'll have the buffalo chicken salad and a Coke Zero," Natalie responded.

"Coming right up." Blessedly, Mrs. Brown left without another word about Jonathan.

After the Texas Cattleman's party, Natalie had been afraid to show her face in town, so she did what she always did when she was stressed: she comfort-ate ice cream and ordered Chinese and pizza and kept to herself the last two weeks. She even ignored Chelsea's calls. Consequently, she gained five pounds.

After Natalie saw the scale ticking in the wrong direction, she knew she had to shake off this depression and get on with life. So what if she lived out her worst embarrassment in front of the town? She would take it on the chin and move forward.

It wasn't, however, easy to forget her infatuation with Jonathan Lattimore. Why? Because when she was thirteen, Jonathan saved her from a band of bullies who relentlessly teased her about being overweight. Although he'd been a few years older than Natalie, he'd been kind and it had meant the world to a young girl with poor self-esteem. Natalie quietly tracked him over the years, which was made easier since Chelsea's family and the Lattimores were neighbors and close friends.

As the years went by, her admiration led to a healthy

dose of lust, especially when at sixteen she began working at the diner. Jonathan would come in with the ranch hands and he looked so darn sexy in his jeans and plaid shirt that Natalie's heart went pitter-pat. If she was on shift, she always made sure he got an extra-large piece of pie. Peach was his favorite, too. And she knew he liked gravy over his french fries and didn't like onions but loved pickles on his cheeseburgers.

God, what's wrong with me? Natalie thought.

She was embarrassed that everyone learned during the livestream that she had a crush on Jonathan. She'd told Chelsea that "Jonathan is the most amazing man I've ever met. I can see myself with him because he would make a great husband and father." Chelsea had been shocked by her confession. She hadn't realized the depth of Natalie's feelings.

Chelsea and Jonathan grew up together because their ranches bordered each other. Both families were powerful and wealthy, the Royal elite. Natalie often saw Jonathan at social engagements she went to with Chelsea, but he'd never shown any interest in her. When Natalie came home after her freshman year in college twenty pounds lighter, she had been ready to go after what she wanted. Instead, she discovered Jonathan had married. She felt like the rug had been pulled out from under her, but surprisingly his marriage hadn't lasted long. Natalie thought she might be the woman to help heal his broken heart, or so she'd hoped, but in the years since his divorce, Jonathan had become a workaholic and rarely dated. And so her feelings remained unrequited and hidden—until last month.

The glass doors of the diner swung open moments later and to her dismay, Jonathan walked in *alone*. A convulsive shiver ran down her spine as she stared at him. He looked like a double scoop of Ben & Jerry's chocolate ice cream in faded jeans, a crisp white shirt, a Stetson and his famous well-worn cowboy boots.

What was it about this man that spoke to her every female mating instinct and made her want to have his babies? Perhaps it was his height. At six foot two, Jonathan towered over her own five foot seven inches. Or was it his taut, sexy butt outlined in those jeans? Jonathan was no stranger to physical labor, having worked on his family's ranch his entire life. Or maybe it was his sinfully sexy lips and hella fine smile surrounded by a scruffy beard that did the trick? Or was it the sexy Ford F-450 Platinum truck he drove or the opulent ranch-style home that she'd heard from Chelsea was an architectural dream? She'd never been invited, but she would love to see it. Whatever it was, she was drawn to him like catnip.

Quickly, she pulled out her phone and tried to appear engrossed in the device. Would he come over and finally talk to her so they could quash this like two adults? Or would he turn tail and run? Dying to know the answer, she looked up and her nerves leaped in shock when she found his gaze on her. His dark brown eyes were sharp and probing, and panic plunged through Natalie.

Was he going to make a scene? No, that wasn't in Jonathan's character. So why was he staring at her intently as if she knew the secrets of the universe, which she absolutely did not? She needed to do something. She had to take control of her own fate and when she was about to get up, Mrs. Brown came strolling back with her buffalo chicken salad.

"Here you go, darling." Mrs. Brown laid the delicious-looking salad in front of Natalie with a flourish. "Hope you enjoy it."

"Thank you." Natalie slid out from the booth, but when she did, Jonathan was already gone. She glanced around the diner, but he wasn't there. Just then, she heard the slow rumble of a truck outside and rushed out the door to see Jonathan pull away from the curb.

So he was taking the "turn tail and run" approach. Just great! Natalie huffed and walked back to her seat. This standoff between them had to come to a stop, but if Jonathan refused to talk to her, she would respect his wishes. She would focus on work instead and clearing her plate before her upcoming vacation. Picking up her phone, she glanced at the calendar. One week until her trip to Galveston. And it couldn't come fast enough.

Damn. Why had he done that? Jonathan Lattimore thought as he pulled out of the Royal Diner's parking lot and edged onto Main Street. Because he couldn't bear to see the hopeful look in Natalie Hastings's eyes. As soon as he walked in and saw her, he'd been unable to look away.

Natalie was every man's wet dream. She had a voluptuous figure with a behind and full breasts. Her face was angelic and encompassed by big brown eyes, a pert nose and kissable lips. He'd always thought she was attractive, but dating someone so close to home was a no-no for him. After his divorce from Anne, he'd kept his relationships casual, but Natalie? She was the type of woman you got serious about. And he was done with commitment. Marriage to Anne had been one of the worst mistakes of his life and their split was acrimonious. The entire fiasco had done a real number on his head. Made him doubt himself and not trust members of the opposite sex. Consequently, he refused to ever marry again.

He'd always known Natalie had a crush on him, but he'd kept her at arm's length even though they had a lot of the same friends in town. She was friends with Chelsea Grandin, whom he'd known since childhood. But last month, everything came to a head when he heard her voice through the speakers at the Texas Cattleman's party. Her sweet declaration of how she thought he was amazing and could see herself with him because he would make a great husband and was father material had been disconcerting because Natalie had no idea who he really was. He wasn't deserving of her—or anyone's—admiration.

If Natalie really knew him, she'd run in the opposite direction and never look back, just like his former wife, Anne, had done. Anne told him he was a workaholic with no time for a spouse. Said he loved the land more than her. When all he was trying to do was expand his family's legacy. Anne hadn't understood. She'd told him he was cold, unfeeling, and incapable of loving and caring for another human being. Maybe she was right. They'd both been unhappy in the marriage and were thankful when it ended so they could go their separate ways.

Jonathan wasn't interested in dipping his feet into those muddy waters again. The divorce weighed heavily on him, and he'd been unable to let go of the pain. He felt responsible that he couldn't make it work and that his ex-wife had been forced to do the unthinkable without even telling him. The guilt ate at Jonathan. He must be a horrible human being if she felt she had to do that to them. So when he saw Natalie at the diner moments ago, he did the only thing he could—he ran as fast as his long legs could carry him. He didn't want to give her false hope there could ever be more between them.

Out of his rearview mirror, he saw her exit the diner and watch him flee. He knew he was being a coward by not facing her, but he wasn't altogether certain he could do the gentlemanly thing if the situation ever presented itself for them to get to know each other. Hearing her spoken declaration of her desire for more between them was tempting. It made him want to throw caution to the wind and take her up on the unspoken offer in her eyes and lose himself between her thighs.

Jesus, he had to get his mind out of the gutter. He was due to meet his parents this evening. He'd gone to the diner so he could bring dessert. Instead, he would come empty-handed because he'd been afraid to face a beautiful, sexy woman in a figure-hugging maxi dress. He was hoping the dinner wouldn't be about Heath Thurston's claim that the oil rights on the Lattimore and Grandin ranches belonged to him. Both families had devoted a lot of time and energy to uncovering the truth. Jonathan didn't believe it for a second. There was no way his grandfather would give up rights to their land to an outsider. Jonathan wasn't about to let Heath come in and take what was theirs. He would fight for his legacy.

When he pulled his Ford F-450 into the Lattimore family ranch a half hour later, it was nearly sunset. It was one of his favorite times of day. He loved to sit on his parents' wraparound porch and watch the sunset across the vast horizon that was the Lattimore ranch. The ranch comprised hundreds of acres that had been in his family for generations, and was now at risk because of Thurston's claim against them.

Turning off the ignition, he headed inside. He found his parents in the living room of the sprawling five-bedroom, two-story home. They were seated on the sofa. His father, Ben Lattimore, was in his usual button-down shirt and dark-washed jeans. His hair was short and trimmed with bits of salt and pepper. His mother Barbara Lattimore's jet-black hair was styled in a chic bob, and she had on a tunic and palazzo pants. Jonathan favored her with his rich honey-brown complexion.

"Hey, Mom." Jonathan walked forward and leaned

down to plant a kiss on her cheek. "Dad." He gave him a quick one-armed hug.

"Jonathan, I'm so glad you could make it," his mother replied, putting down the book she'd been reading. "Please have a seat."

Jonathan's mouth curled into a frown as he sat across from them in an adjacent chair. "Have I done something wrong? I feel like I've been called to the principal's office."

Both of his parents looked very serious and Jonathan wondered if they were worried about him. He knew he had been putting in a lot of hours for a long time now. He'd used the divorce as an excuse, but then the oil claim came up. There always seemed to be a need for a little extra man power.

His father let out a big belly laugh. "Nothing so dire, son, but it has come to our attention how many hours you've been working at the ranch."

"There's a lot to be done." There was a dizzying array of activities to keep their horse and cattle ranch in operation. Their father was general manager. Jonathan handled the office administration as well as sharing operational duties with his younger brother, Jayden. His sister Alexa was an attorney and was handling the oil case for the Grandins and Lattimores.

There wasn't any friction between the Lattimores like there was with their friends. The Grandins were in disagreement over who would take over the ranch one day. Although he was eldest, Jonathan was happy to have someone to split the workload with.

"True, there's a lot to do," his mother said, "but you

don't know when to stop and smell the roses. That's where we—" she glanced at her husband "—come in."

Jonathan leaned back and regarded them. "I get the feeling I'm not going to like what you have to say."

"We've paid for a week's vacation for you in Galveston," his mother responded. She stood up and handed him an envelope.

"Vacation?" Jonathan said as if it were a dirty four-letter word.

"Yes, *vacation*," his father reiterated with a smirk. "You need one. You've been working much too many hours and it's time you took it easy and let someone else do the heavy lifting."

"That's not necessary, Dad," Jonathan said, sitting forward. "I've got things handled."

"We know you do," his mother said softly. "And this isn't some sort of punishment, Jonathan, but ever since you divorced Anne, you've become a workaholic, never taking time for yourself."

"I take time when I need to."

His father folded his arms across his chest and asked, "When was the last time you took a day off?" When Jonathan began to speak, he added, "And not because you were sick, which you rarely are."

Jonathan paused and had to think about the question. He couldn't recall the last time he had any sort of *real* vacation. Since the oil claim, he'd been busier researching the case with Alexa, all the while keeping himself busy so he could forget about Natalie's confession and not be tempted to take their relationship to a more personal level. "All right, fine. I admit I've been a bit busy."

"Then you'll admit you need some time off to recharge the batteries," his mother responded.

"And before you say anything, you should know that this isn't a request," his father stated, looking him dead in the eye. "We are ordering you to go on vacation. Your mother has already taken the liberty of paying for a full week at the resort."

"But, Dad…"

"It's a done deal, Jonathan," his father replied. "Now how about we eat one of your mother's delicious meals."

"Sure, but where's everyone else?" Jonathan inquired.

"Caitlin and Alexa are having a double date with their fiancés, Dev and Jackson. I think they are talking wedding shop. And as for Jayden, you know your brother likes the ladies," their father responded.

Jonathan laughed. He would have loved some reinforcements to help convince their parents to change their mind, but he was on his own.

Reluctantly, Jonathan left his parents' home a couple of hours later. He wasn't happy about the forced vacation. There was a lot on his plate, but he couldn't deny his parents had a point. When was the last time he'd taken some real time away from the ranch?

Too long.

Maybe while he was away, he would find a beautiful lady to spend some time with. In bed later that night, Jonathan dreamed of a curvaceous woman twining her legs around him as he thrust deep into her body.

The passionate entanglement sent fireworks exploding through Jonathan's chest and he wanted more. As she came into focus, he realized who it was he craved.

Dammit.

Natalie Hastings.

Two

Ohmigod, it can't be him, Natalie thought, rolling her luggage behind the tall column of the beachfront Galveston resort. Peeking around the column, she had another look.

Crap! It is.

Of all the places in Texas, Jonathan Lattimore had to show up at her vacation spot?

He stood at the reception desk casually dressed in black jeans and a white T-shirt that perfectly accentuated his tall, athletic frame. Even in profile from where she stood, there was no doubt how handsome he was and strongly male. Damn her heart for beating so madly because he was a few feet away.

Natalie wanted him—had always wanted him, but how could she feel this way for a man who didn't want to talk to her so much, he'd done an about-face at the diner? She was trying to get away from the embarrassment and the humiliation of everyone knowing about her unrequited feelings. She constantly wondered if they were judging her again as they had in her youth. Why would a man as handsome, educated and powerful as Jonathan Lattimore ever want her? Natalie was ashamed of her behavior and desperately wanted a do-over, but in life you didn't get one. So she'd come to Galveston for a change of scenery and to stop thinking about Jonathan Lattimore. Natalie slapped her hand against her forehead.

What am I going to do? There was nowhere for her to run without Jonathan seeing her. She had to stay hidden. Glancing nervously around, she saw the concierge walking in her direction and quickly motioned the bespectacled man over.

"Ma'am? Is there something I can help you with? Do you need a bellboy for your luggage?" the older man inquired, inclining his head to her Louis Vuitton luggage behind the column. The luggage had been a special treat Natalie purchased after her company, H & W Marketing, took off.

"No, no." Natalie shook her head. "I need to change hotels. Do you have a sister hotel perhaps where I can rebook my stay?"

"I'm not sure if there's availability, ma'am, but I can certainly inquire for you," he responded. "Why don't you have a drink at the pool bar while I try to sort this out for you?"

A drink was exactly what she could use right now, Natalie thought. "That sounds lovely, thank you."

The concierge reached for the handle of her luggage. "I'll take your bag and put it in storage while you wait."

Natalie nodded, releasing the handle she had a death grip on. She hazarded another glance from behind the column and saw Jonathan walking toward the elevator. If he was headed to his room, it would give her plenty of time to figure out her next move, because there was no way in hell she was staying in the same resort as Jonathan Lattimore.

After the concierge took her bag and the coast was clear, Natalie shuffled down the hall toward the sign pointing to the pool. She would drown her sorrows in a very strong margarita and pray the hotel gods would shine down and offer her a get-out-of-jail card.

Jonathan didn't want to be here. If he had his druthers, he would be back on the Lattimore family ranch in Royal. He was a country boy through and through. He had no idea what he was supposed to do in a sleepy beach town for a week, but his parents had given him no option.

They paid for an all-expenses vacation, and he was damn well going to take it because he'd need to be strong to fight Heath Thurston's claim. His family ranch was at stake. The ranch meant everything to him. It was his birthright. His grandfather Augustus Lattimore handed the reins to his son Ben, and his father would do the same to Jonathan one day. He wasn't about to let an interloper come in and take what was his. Jonathan had sacrificed a lot, including his marriage, to ensure the ranch would continue for generations.

He dropped his luggage in the lavishly furnished suite complete with a king-size bed, large living room and dining area, fully stocked wet bar, and luxurious bathroom. Then he walked over to one of two balconies that overlooked the Gulf of Mexico. This was more like it. He wasn't used to being indoors. He was an outdoors kind of guy, and he was in desperate need of a beer.

Jonathan wondered if this bourgeois hotel even offered a good beer or whether they were all about expertly crafted cocktails. He intended to find out. Although he hadn't been primed for a vacation, Jonathan had to admit getting away from prying eyes in Royal wasn't a bad idea. Ever since the TCC party last month, folks had been gossiping about him and he didn't like it.

Even Alexa had gotten into the mix, asking him if he'd spoken to Natalie and pushing him to call her. *To say what?* A conversation would be awkward for them both. It was better to just let the whole thing blow over. Eventually, everyone would find something or *someone else* to talk about. He, however, couldn't stop thinking about Natalie and how earnest she'd been about her feelings. Like most men, he wasn't one for laying his feelings bare; he kept things close to the vest. But Natalie, she had him tied up in knots.

Right now, he was going to go find that beer.

Natalie had to admit she'd chosen well. She was in marketing, after all, and research was her middle name.

The resort's pool lived up to the hype. It was adorned in soothing shades of white and coral and was exactly the chic coastal hideaway she'd envisioned when she thought about lounging poolside on a sun lounger in one of the many bathing suits she bought. She'd even let Chelsea talk her into purchasing not one but *two* bikinis. Was her best friend the reason Jonathan was in Galveston? No, Chelsea wouldn't do something like that without discussing it with her first.

As a curvy woman with large breasts and wide hips, Natalie didn't do two-piece swimwear. But Chelsea, who was tall as she was willowy, told her, "If you've got it, flaunt it." So Natalie decided to go for it. Would she even get the chance to wear the bikini? Or enjoy the outdoor firepit and watch the sun set in the Gulf? Not if Jonathan Lattimore was here.

Why, oh why was this happening to her? She was a good person. She helped the elderly, volunteered at an orphanage and liked puppies. Why had fate conspired against her to reveal her deepest darkest secret?

She was so nervous about his presence at the hotel, she was drinking her second margarita. It had taken the edge off after discovering Jonathan at the same resort. After calling the concierge every fifteen minutes, he just informed her he was unable to locate another room at one of their sister hotels. Instead, he'd come to the pool bar, given Natalie her key card and asked if she would like her luggage taken to her room. She had no choice but to say yes; she wasn't going to forgo her stay. Damn! She would stay and take the risk; somehow, she would weather the embarrassment if she ran into Jonathan.

"Can I get a beer?" Natalie heard Jonathan's voice seconds before her eyes landed on him two stools away at the bar. The bar was nearly empty because the happy hour crowd had gone in for dinner. With the exception of the bartender, it was the two of them. *Alone.*

No, no, no. She hadn't had enough margaritas yet.

Plastering a fake smile on her face, she spun around on her stool to face Jonathan and like always her heart lurched at his sexy features. Perhaps she should act as if she didn't know him? No, he would see the ploy a mile away. She decided on the direct approach. "Jonathan? What are *you* doing here?"

"Natalie?" The surprise in Jonathan's voice was evident because he stumbled off the bar stool but righted himself before he fell.

Natalie couldn't help chuckling. "Umm… Are you okay?"

"I was hoping you didn't notice that," Jonathan said, attempting a smile.

She chuckled nervously. "Sorry, but I did. Anyway, I'm here on vacation. How about you?" She tried not to look at his thick lips, which she was certain he knew how to use to make a woman want to drop her panties.

"Same."

One-word answers. *That* wasn't good. She felt as awkward as he did. If he'd just cleared the air after the TCC event, they'd be on better footing.

"I should get going." She rose with her margarita in

hand and was shocked when Jonathan placed one of his large hands on her arm. "Stay. Have a drink with me."

Her brow furrowed. "Are you sure?" Wasn't she the last person he wanted to spend time with? He'd done a good job of avoiding her the last month since the party and let's not mention the diner when he rushed *away* from her. Natalie got the hint, loud and clear.

"Of course." He inclined his head.

"Very well." Natalie plopped herself back down on the bar stool she'd been about to vacate and peered into her drink. She was going to need another one of these if she had to sit next to her not-so-secret crush. She motioned to the bartender for another margarita.

"So…" Jonathan moved closer onto the empty bar stool beside her. "Will your friend or—" his voice trailed off for a moment "—or someone else mind us having a drink together?"

Was that his coy way of asking if she came to Galveston alone? If so, he wasn't very good at it. "I'm here alone if that's what you're asking," Natalie responded evenly.

He nodded and gave a small smile. "I was. Do you normally vacation alone?"

"Not usually, but in this instance, I needed to get away from Royal."

He was silent for several moments, as if he didn't know why she had to get out of Dodge, but then to her astonishment he said, "It'll all die down in a few weeks. No one will even remember what you said."

It was the first time Jonathan acknowledged he heard the live recording. Natalie didn't know how to react to his casual reference to the single most embarrassing moment of her life. She was surprised he didn't think she was a stalker being at the same resort as him.

Instead of responding to Jonathan's statement, Natalie ignored it. Wasn't that why she was here? She was attempting to put the past behind her and move forward, but that was hard to do when the object of your affection was sitting right next to you. In her wildest dreams, she never imagined they would be sitting side by side sharing a drink after the humiliation she suffered a month ago. The pitiful looks she received since then from everyone in town had been bad enough, but to have Jonathan actively avoid her had been the worst.

"I doubt that. Tongues have a tendency to wag in Royal."

"Listen, I appreciate all the nice things you said about me, but if it's all the same to you, I'd like to forget it. Put in the past. Can you do that?"

She nodded.

"Good, because I'm interested in some R & R and discovering Galveston. How about you?"

"Same."

"So let's toast." Jonathan held up his beer bottle. "To taking it easy."

They clinked beverages. "To taking it easy."

Jonathan couldn't believe Natalie Hastings was in Galveston. When he had thought about how this week would go, he would never have predicted this fine-ass woman would be sitting next to him. Natalie was sexy as hell in a floral halter jumpsuit with a deep V-neck showing off the swell of her full cleavage. An electric charge hit his groin.

He'd always known Natalie had a crush on him, but until he heard the audio, he didn't realize it was more than a silly crush. She wasn't staring at him, although he wished she would, so he could drown in her dark brown orbs. Her hair was an intricate updo of braids and showed off her face. After the erotic dream he'd had about her, Jonathan shifted uncomfortably in his seat. Having Natalie up close and personal would test even the holiest man's resolve. Every inch of his body throbbed with awareness. Which was the exact opposite of forgetting about her. Maybe in order to move on, he would have to burn out this attraction between them? That sounded like fun. And wasn't that what a vacation was all about?

"How long are you staying?" Jonathan inquired.

"A week."

"Me, too. Not by choice. My parents forced this vacation on me. Told me I'm a workaholic and to take time to smell the roses."

"Are they right?"

Jonathan shrugged. "I don't think so." He was fine with his life. He lived and worked on the multimillion-dollar ranch he loved that had been in his family for generations. He turned to look at Natalie and she looked as if she didn't believe him. "Sounds like you think they're right."

"I only know what I see," Natalie replied.

"Which is?"

"Every time I see you in town, you're on ranch business. Do you ever take time for yourself? To do something for fun?"

He had some fun ideas for this week. All of them included Natalie in his bed.

"Don't you ever get lonely?"

Jonathan was silent. He was comfortable with his solitary existence. If he did want company, he went for long rides on his favorite horse, or he called one of his lady friends for hot sex. It worked, but his family seemed to think he was stuck in a rut. Maybe he was. He hadn't always been this way. Before Anne, he'd been more social and enjoyed spending time with family and friends. After the divorce, he'd become closed-off and guarded.

"Everyone needs somebody, Jonathan."

Jonathan leaned away from Natalie. Her comment made him think of his ex-wife, Anne, who thought he was a workaholic, an unfeeling and cold bastard, but it wasn't true. Even though he regretted the decision afterward, when they'd married, he'd fancied himself in love, but she wasn't the woman for him. She was needy and clingy, wanting Jonathan all to herself. Anne wanted the status of being married to a Lattimore and when she realized that equated to some lonely days while he worked, she cut her losses. Jonathan wondered if she ever really loved him at all.

He blinked rapidly, focusing back on the current conversation with Natalie, but she was pulling several bills from her purse and throwing them on the bar. "If you'll excuse me," she said, and quickly exited.

"Natalie, wait!" Had he done something to offend her? But she was already several yards away. He slipped a twenty from his billfold and slid it onto the bar. Then he was rushing after Natalie. He didn't want their evening to end like this. Although he hadn't planned it, he didn't want to let this feeling of anticipation go and he wasn't about to let her go, either.

Three

Natalie couldn't believe she'd been foolish enough to think she could sit beside Jonathan Lattimore and have a drink like they were two normal strangers meeting on a holiday. This wasn't *Roman Holiday*. *I'm such an idiot. He probably thinks my comment about everyone needing someone was some sort of come-on attempt. That* I *want to be the* somebody *he needs*.

As much as she might wish that were true, it wasn't. She had to face the facts. Jonathan Lattimore would *never* be interested in her other than as a passing acquaintance. The sooner she got over the romantic notions that they would make a great couple, the better.

Once she reached the hotel lobby, she glanced around for the elevators and furiously pressed the up button. She heard Jonathan calling out after her, but she didn't stop walking. She wasn't interested in anything he had to say. She wanted to get to her room, have a hot shower and figure out how she would stay out of his path for the rest of the week. Because why should she leave? She paid for this trip and had as much a right to be here as him. She wasn't about to let him run her off.

The elevator arrived several seconds later, but it wasn't fast enough.

"Natalie!" Jonathan called her name and within seconds, he'd caught up to her.

She glared at him before entering the cab. Natalie thought her withering look would be enough to deter him, but he joined her anyway. The silence inside the short climb to the third floor was deafening. She certainly wasn't about to apologize for attempting to care about him, but he wasn't easy to ignore, either. With his commanding stature and presence, he seemed to take up all the oxygen in the cab.

When the elevator dinged on her floor, Natalie quickly exited and rushed down the hall, but Jonathan's sure steps followed. Reaching her door, she swiped the key card and was about to open it when she found Jonathan behind her. She turned and faced him. "What do you want?"

"If you'll give me the chance, I'd like to apologize," Jonathan replied.

Natalie was shocked. She hadn't expected that response and felt like someone had let the wind out of her sails. So much for righteous indignation.

"Can I come in?" Jonathan asked, peering at her intently.

Natalie didn't know why, but she held open the door. As Jonathan walked past her, she caught a tantalizing whiff of his sexy scent that was male and earthy with a hint of spice. Everything about him assailed her senses, and it made her think of all sorts of naughty things she'd like to do with him. She shook her head to erase the image and shut the door.

Walking inside, she was impressed with the corner suite the concierge had given her. A big bed stood center stage and there was a small, nicely appointed seating area with a desk. The curtains were open, and she could see a balcony. But nothing was more impressive than the six-foot-plus man standing in the middle of the room dominating the space.

Although he was broad-shouldered and slim-hipped, there was an inherent strength in his gait and Natalie found herself unable to look away. Jonathan fit the mold for tall, dark and handsome.

"I'm sorry, Natalie," Jonathan began. "I guess I don't know to act around a lady anymore. I'm sorry if I appeared standoffish because that wasn't my intent. I got caught up in some past memories."

Natalie shrugged as she slipped her purse off her shoulder and placed it on the cocktail table. "It happens sometimes."

He cocked his head to one side as if he didn't believe her. "Are you being real with me? Or telling me what I want to hear, so I'll get out of your room?"

"I'm being straight up. I accept your apology." She took a seat on the sofa.

"Good. Because I enjoyed talking to you downstairs and I don't want that to be our last conversation."

"You don't?" She didn't understand what was happening. Jonathan always treated her as if she were a friend and nothing more. Did he see this vacation as a way to deepen their relationship? She'd always wanted that, but she didn't want to be used, either. He knew how she felt about him. It would be easy for him to lay on the charm. She had to be on her guard.

He shook his head. "No, I want to get to know you better. Can we start over?"

"I suppose," Natalie said uneasily. Her mouth was dry, and her knees were weak, so she kicked off her sandals. She didn't know what to do next; there was a palpable energy pulsating back and forth between them. "Umm...would you like a drink?"

"I'd like that very much." Jonathan's eyes met her gaze with a directness that stole her breath.

Natalie blinked, snapping her out of the spiderlike web she felt he had her in. "I have no idea what's in the fridge."

"Why don't we find out?" His voice was like dark chocolate and red wine, rich and full-bodied, full of flavor. She watched him walk over and bend his tall frame to peer into the mini fridge. From her viewpoint, Natalie saw some water, Coke, mini spirits, and small orange and cranberry juices, but she would much rather focus on his bum in his jeans.

Jonathan pulled out several beverages and made a screwdriver for her and a rum and Coke for him. Afterward, he came down and sat beside her on the sofa.

She was surprised when he asked, "Have you heard anything about Aubrey Collins?" She doubted he was here for conversation. Or was that the excuse he was going to use for his being in her room?

Nonetheless, she answered his question. "Last I heard, she's suffered some memory loss," Natalie replied, "though the doctors are hopeful it's temporary."

Aubrey was a mutual friend who'd been injured at the Texas Cattleman's Club party a month ago when the podium she was standing on collapsed. When she fell, she'd hit her head and was knocked unconscious.

"I'm sorry to hear that," Jonathan said, sipping his drink. "I hope she recovers."

"So do I," Natalie responded. She also prayed they moved on from this topic of conversation, but her prayers weren't answered.

"Are we ever going to talk about the elephant in the room?" Jonathan inquired, turning to his side. His eyes narrowed and he raked her face with his gaze.

"Why?" Natalie's pulse leaped and she found herself ensnared by the look he was giving her. "I want to forget that day ever happened. Plus we agreed to start over. Why dwell in the past?"

"Because it's necessary to move forward," Jonathan responded. "Listen." One of his large hands grasped one of her thighs and Natalie sucked in a deep breath at the unexpected contact. A jolt hit her like an electrical charge reverberating lower, and her core tightened in response. "I was flattered when I heard how you felt about me even though your feelings might be misguided."

She frowned. "You were flattered? Then why did you avoid me?"

Jonathan shrugged. "Because I didn't know what to say. I'm really not all that great."

Natalie burst out laughing and suddenly the ice was broken between them. All this time, she'd been so worried to face him, but she could forget her humiliation when he was self-deprecating. "Thanks for that," she said. "I think I've been taking this way too seriously and I guess we could both learn to lighten up."

"Yeah, we could."

Natalie looked up and found Jonathan's caramel-colored eyes, rimmed with thick, curling lashes, looking at her intently in a way she'd never seen before. They stared at each other for several long, compelling seconds. It set her pulse racing and Natalie had to remind herself that Jonathan wasn't interested in her. In the past, she might have thrown herself at him, but this time he would have to make the first move. And…there was something dangerous in his stare.

Jonathan should have never come to her room. After being shocked to see Natalie at the pool bar, he should have walked in the other direction, but there was something about her. About the way she looked at him so sweetly that made a flare of desire run through him. His gaze swept her face, and he knew she registered his interest.

Did it surprise her? It shouldn't. Her body was perfect in every way to him. It's why he hadn't removed his hand from her thigh. He'd given in to the impulse to touch her and if given the slightest indication she wanted more, he would touch her all over from her generous breasts all the way down to her petite feet.

Her eyes were fastened on his and Jonathan felt the throb of sexual energy pulsating between them, dimming out anything but the two of them. He reached out his hand and slowly trailed a path down the curve of her cheek. She was as entranced as he was, so when he curved his hand around the nape of her neck and brought her toward him, she came willingly. Seconds later, his mouth closed over hers and an urgency he'd never felt before rushed to the surface. When he coaxed her lips apart, to deepen the kiss, she obliged. So Jonathan held Natalie in place and plundered her mouth, but even that wasn't enough.

He pulled her closer and only then did he give in to temptation to shape her breasts. He splayed his hands over them, and they ripened at his touch. When her nipple crested against his palm, Jonathan wanted to feast on it, but this was Natalie. She had feelings for him. He didn't want to hurt her or have her confused by what this was. Lust pure and simple.

Reluctantly, he pulled away and tried to regain his composure. "That was a revelation." His voice sounded low and husky even to him. Because if he was honest, he wanted to stay the night with Natalie and lose himself in all her delicious curves, but it wouldn't be fair.

It wasn't a surprise to her, Natalie thought. Although she was taken off guard, her lips had parted when he moved his ferociously over them and she greedily wanted more. Because deep down she'd always known it could be good between them, but she never had the opportunity to explore the attraction she sensed might be there. Now, she knew, it hadn't been completely one-sided. At the very least, he desired her.

"Are you about to apologize for kissing me?" Natalie asked. She wasn't sure she could bear it because she had been lost in his drugging kisses.

He shook his head. "No, I've been wanting to do that for a long time."

A slow smile crept across her face. If she wasn't careful, Jonathan could break down all her layers of defense. But there was no way she was going to turn back from the one chance she had to have her heart's desire. So she said, "What happens in Galveston, stays in Galveston."

That seemed to be all the encouragement Jonathan needed because they came toward each other once again. They kissed, their mouths fusing, and he pulled her into him. Natalie was breathless, but she didn't care. Jonathan ignited a furnace inside her and she was engulfed in the heat, in the heat of him. When she felt his hand behind her neck unclipping the snap of her jumpsuit, she welcomed it, especially when it slid slowly down her trembling body.

It seemed she'd waited a lifetime for this moment, and she didn't want to miss a single minute. She raised her hands behind her and unclasped her bra, letting it fall to the floor.

"God, you're beautiful." Jonathan's voice was raspy as his eyes devoured her naked bosom. "I can't wait to see all of you." He took her by the hand and pulled her off the sofa so the rest of the garment could fall to the floor.

Although there was a niggling worry in the back of her mind that he could be using her for sex, this felt right and she refused to talk herself out of it. It was a dream come true to be in Jonathan's arms, and she wanted him. Jonathan wanted her, too, because he was feasting his eyes on her, and she let him right before she lifted her hands to loosen the topknot of her intricate updo. Her braids fell in a cloud around her shoulders. Jonathan wasn't motionless any longer and pulled her firmly to him. Natalie felt his hard length against her middle as he claimed her mouth and kissed her once more with the same rabid hunger he had before.

Natalie went up in flames in his arms and rational thought evaporated in a groan of craving. Desire surged and she couldn't wait to help divest Jonathan of his clothes, which were an impediment to her feeling all of him. She wanted his naked flesh against her skin. Once his clothes were flung aside, Jonathan half carried her to the bed, yanking back the covers to lay her feverish body against the cool sheets.

"Natalie." He gazed down at her, and she knew she had to look crazed with desire. She lifted her arms, welcoming him, and he came down on top of her. His kiss was hot, hungry and urgent, drugging her and pulling her deeper into a carnal spell where her very existence was reduced to this moment with him.

And she gave as good as she got, pulling and tugging Jonathan's tongue into her mouth again and again.

But then he broke the kiss to trail hot kisses down her nape, shoulder and lower until he came to her breasts. He worshipped the full mounds, sweeping his tongue over the cresting brown peaks. Natalie cried out at the hot, sucking heat of his mouth and clasped his head to her bosom. She wished she could keep him there forever, but instead he went questing further, down over her abdomen until he came to her panties.

Hooking his thumb, he pulled the silky material past her thighs and lower until he could fling it away. Then he sat back on his haunches and looked at her. Usually this was when Natalie was self-conscious about her figure, but not with Jonathan. There was a naked hunger in his eyes that she'd never seen with another man. She could only watch as he lowered himself to the bed and pushed her thighs apart to nuzzle at the dark vee of her arousal.

She sucked in a breath when he pressed open-mouthed kisses to her thick thighs. And as she felt his breath get closer and closer to the center of her, she squirmed, but he put a hand on her belly, holding her still.

"I've got you," he rasped. Then he was reaching underneath her to grasp her bottom and pull her forward to his waiting mouth. Natalie bucked at the feel of having his tongue on the secret folds of her damp flesh, but he didn't stop there. He used his fingers to thoroughly explore every inch of her, eliciting more and more pleasure. It was bliss beyond her wildest dreams. Tension began spiraling deep inside as Jonathan took her to new heights that had her legs shaking. When he delved deep and flicked his tongue on the right spot, Natalie's world exploded, and she saw stars.

She was vaguely aware of Jonathan coming back to pay homage to her breasts before moving away for long moments to reach for something. She heard foil rip and then he was back, moving over her and nudging her legs apart. Then in one sure movement, he thrust deep, joining their bodies as one. He took a moment for Natalie to catch her breath. He gave her that time to adjust to his size because he was rather large. As if sensing her discomfort, he pulled out and then slowly eased back in again.

Natalie breathed out.

She felt full. Full of Jonathan. It was amazing, but she wanted more and moved beneath him, letting him know he could go faster. He took the hint and lifted her leg so he could go deeper. Natalie gave a helpless moan of pleasure as he stroked again and again.

She wound her other leg tightly around him and his movements became faster, more urgent. Her skin was growing damp with the need for a release, and she clutched him tightly, clenching her muscles around him. His head was thrown back, and she felt each mind-blowing stroke. He made every cell of her body throb, which told her she was coming near the crest. It didn't take long for another wave of bliss to strike her.

"Oh, yes!" She gave a rapturous exhalation when she toppled over. "Oh yes!" Her orgasm thundered through, shocking her with its intensity. Jonathan reached for her then, giving her the silken thrust of his tongue, teasing and cajoling it with hers until the waves finally eased.

But it wasn't over for Jonathan. His thrust became harder and more urgent until eventually he tensed and gave a shuddering groan as his climax hit. Natalie held him through the storm.

Did he feel as completely undone as she felt?

It had been so potent. So passionate. So necessary.

She moved her hands down his back, listening to his breathing quiet until eventually he moved away from her to lie on his back. She lay beside him utterly exhausted but feeling totally sublime. Her eyes sank shut and she breathed in the male scent of his body as sleep overtook her.

Four

Natalie awoke hours later, or so it seemed. As she eased into consciousness, her mind started remembering the night before. She couldn't believe this was happening. Felt like it was dream. And if it was, it was one she didn't want to wake from. She and Jonathan had made love not once, but twice. After the first time, they made love again hungrily as if they hadn't just had sex. Jonathan had been ravenous and had taken her from the side and behind.

In answer to her memory, there was a dull ache between her legs. She was by no means a virgin, but it had been a couple of years since she'd been intimate with a man. None of them, however, had known how to play her body quite like Jonathan. But then again, she'd never felt about them the way she did him. Speaking of…

She hauled herself upright, clutching the sheet to her bare bosom, and blinked. The bed beside her was empty. She was worrying he may have escaped for the hills, but to her surprise and delight, he emerged from the balcony, clad only in a pair of jeans and carrying a mug that she presumed held coffee. His bare torso was on display and Natalie fought the urge to lick her lips.

In the early-morning hours, she'd run her tongue down every inch of his hairless chest and he loved every minute of it, especially when she went lower and took him into her warm, waiting mouth.

"Good morning, sleepyhead," Jonathan said.

Natalie bent her head and blushed. She didn't usually sleep in. Her eyes momentarily flickered to his. "Why didn't you wake me?"

"You were tired, so I let you sleep." His eyes gleamed softly. He had worn her out the night before with their extracurricular activities. "So, about last night..."

Oh God, here it comes, the morning-after speech. She supposed she should have expected he would have second thoughts, but she hoped not. "As I said last night, what happens here, stays here." She knew he was gun-shy about getting involved.

"Yes, I know, but I rather enjoyed last night," Jonathan replied.

"So did I." She'd never had so many orgasms in one night. It was a heady feeling knowing he knew exactly how to please her without her saying a thing. She'd soared with the butterflies all night long. She would store this night away as a precious memory, an unbelievable dream, so that if it never happened again, she could keep it with her.

"I'm glad." He placed his coffee mug on the nightstand. "It wasn't my intention when I followed you to…"

"Take me to bed?" Natalie offered, gazing up at him with a grin. She needed to do something to ease the uncomfortable look on Jonathan's face. What did he think she was going to do, ask him to marry her or something? She was a twenty-first-century woman and knew how to handle herself, but that didn't mean she wasn't as flummoxed as he was by the unexpected attraction that flared between them.

Jonathan smiled. "That's right." He walked toward her and Natalie couldn't breathe. Everything stopped— her breathing, her heartbeat. She felt like she was suspended in time with Jonathan looking down at her with the strangest expression in his dark eyes.

When he brought his hand up and brushed the tips of his fingers against her lips, a soft sigh escaped her. "You're so lovely…"

Then his head was lowering to hers and Natalie's eyes fluttered shut as he covered her mouth with his. She relished his confident and hungry kiss and wanted it to go on forever. The shape of his lips fit hers and when the tip of his tongue parted her lips, she melted into him. She couldn't help it. It was too good between them, and her body knew it. She released a throaty groan.

Jonathan intuitively understood and leaned her backward onto the bed until she collided with his body.

She *felt* everything. His hot, hard chest, the flat muscles of his abdomen and the proud shape of his erection. Her hand spread over his behind, bringing him exactly where she needed him. His breath hissed and he plundered her mouth, consuming her with his kiss.

His hand rode up her thigh to snatch away the sheet separating them, and Natalie arched her breasts into his chest. When his hand went south and his fingertips unerringly found her plump, aching center and drew the slick folds apart, her breath hitched. When he added another thick finger, her muscles clenched around him. It was pure torture and she moved restlessly against him, desperate to have him fill her.

"Please…" she cried.

He reared back onto his knees and with a primal growl, wrenched off his jeans. He returned to the bed but not before putting on protection over his erection. Then he was back, settling his weight between her parted legs. She hitched her ankles around his waist as he guided himself home in one delicious plunge.

Pure pleasure coursed through her veins. It felt so good having him inside her, filling up every available space. Their mouths locked together as he eased in and out in a delicious rhythm that made her taut with tension. Natalie tried to fight it, but she couldn't, not when his strokes became harder, deeper. He seemed as lost as she to this clawing need for satisfaction. After one final thrust, they reached the pinnacle together and released a long sigh of joy and contentment as they came tumbling back down to earth.

* * *

Jonathan felt a kick in his stomach. He hardly recognized the man he'd become. He'd done it again. Lost his mind in Natalie's arms. When it came to sex, he'd never been insatiable before, but he was inexplicably drawn to Natalie. To the beautiful glow about her and her infectious spirit. So he'd given in to desire and slid his hands beneath the fall of her braids and brought his mouth down on hers. This woman spoke to him and filled every sexual need his libido had and then some. She was his match in every way.

And that was a problem. She had stars in her eyes when it came to him. She didn't know him, not the *real* him. According to his ex, he was a cold and unfeeling bastard and only cared about the ranch. Jonathan was damaged goods and didn't have his whole heart to give to a woman of Natalie's caliber, warm and compassionate.

Emotions warred within him. He had never meant to make love to her, but now that he had, there was no way they could go back to being friends or casual acquaintances. Now he knew she was a real flesh-and-blood female with breasts and a behind that went on for days. She was a woman he could no longer gloss over. It was as if she'd suddenly snapped into existence before his very eyes.

But if she was looking for *more*, he couldn't offer her that. Since Anne, he kiboshed serious relationships. Anne had burned him and Jonathan wasn't altogether sure he'd ever recover from her betrayal. Or that he wanted to. Before *this* went any further, he needed to be sure Natalie understood that.

"Well, that was unexpected," Natalie said, glancing in his direction.

"Yes, my intention was for us to talk and clear the air, so there are no misunderstandings in the future." Jonathan glanced up at the ceiling.

"I understand perfectly," Natalie said, and to his shock, slid away from him, wrapping a sheet around her bosom and standing to face him. "This was a one-time thing." She paused as if considering her words carefully and said, "I mean, it was a one-off. Nothing more."

He frowned. "Is that what you want?"

Natalie cocked her head to one side and regarded him. "You like your solitary life, Jonathan. I get it. I won't disrupt it, not now or in Royal."

Jonathan sat upright, pushing several pillows behind him. "I appreciate that…" His voice trailed off. He hadn't been anticipating her easy reception. He thought she would want more from him than he was willing or capable of giving.

"Is there a 'but' in there somewhere?" Natalie asked.

"We're both here for the week…"

Natalie nodded and understanding crossed her features. She somehow knew what he was asking without him having to say it. "I'm open to a no-strings-attached vacation fling if you are."

"Really?"

"You sound surprised."

"You're just…"

"The kind of girl you marry?" Natalie inquired. "Us nice girls know how to have fun, too. We're not all waiting for a man to put a ring on it."

Jonathan chuckled. "I suppose that was presumptuous of me."

"Yeah, it was. So what's it going to be?" She put her hands on her wide hips.

"It's going to be a hell yes!" Jonathan roared. "Now get back in this bed and let's pick up where we left off." He held the duvet open and to his surprise and delight, Natalie tossed the sheet and slid in beside him so he could gorge himself yet again.

As she sat across from Jonathan at one of the famous seafood houses on Galveston's pier, Natalie's mind was reeling. Reeling from the whirlwind of emotions she'd experienced the last twenty-four hours. The shock and disbelief that Jonathan Lattimore, the beautiful, sexy rancher she'd crushed on for as long as she could remember, was her lover—and not for one night as she'd thought when she woke up this morning, but for the entire week! Although she was ready for more, she was willing to accept this time with Jonathan because she'd always wanted him and this week allowed her the opportunity to live out her fantasies.

Natalie felt as if someone had truly sprinkled fairy dust over her and brought her in full Technicolor to Jonathan. She'd been nervous dressing for the evening, but eventually she settled on a blush off-the-shoulder cap-sleeve dress with a ruffle detail from the waist to the knee. Why was she nervous? Because he was looking at her. Truly looking at her for the first time. Hell, he hadn't just looked, either. He'd kissed, licked, touched, tasted every inch of her until she was putty in his hands. When he mentioned they were going to be here the week, she realized he wanted a fling while they were in Galveston. She had enjoyed their night and morning together. Was it wrong to want it to last for a little bit longer? It was risky because of her long-held feelings, but it was worth it.

"What would you like to eat?" Jonathan asked, disturbing her wayward thoughts.

Natalie swallowed. "Umm, I don't know." Her eyes glossed over the menu. She quickly rattled off something and while Jonathan ordered, she simply drank him in. He'd showered and changed into black pants and a black silk button-down shirt. He looked scrumptious! When he ordered appetizers and a bottle of Dom Pérignon, she raised a brow.

"I'm hungry, woman, you wore me out." Jonathan gave her a smile. The way it altered the planes of his face made a whole flock of butterflies swarm in her belly. "I need sustenance so I'll be ready for night two."

Natalie blushed. She wasn't used to the intense physical intimacy they shared. At first their conversation was a bit stilted. She felt awkward and could only respond with short phrases. When he asked her about her job and if she enjoyed it that's when Natalie blossomed. She shared how she and her partner, Brent White, got started, opening the firm with a small investment from both of their families. Her grandparents believed in Natalie's dream and wanted to help in any way they could. Once she and Brent found a space in town, they were on their way.

She was thankful when the waiter returned with the champagne because it gave her something to do other than stare at Jonathan. As her flute gradually emptied, Natalie found she could relax and enjoy the evening.

Jonathan loved talking about the ranch and the latest innovations they were making to help the cattle operation run smoother. They also bred horses, which they sold to private owners and polo players.

"You're very passionate about ranching."

"It's in my blood," Jonathan said, sipping his champagne, "and it's what we Lattimores have been doing for generations."

"You're lucky to have a close family," Natalie replied. "I'm envious."

He leaned back and looked at her. "Why is that?"

Natalie shrugged. "Because it's always been me and my grandparents. My mother wasn't interested in being a parent, at least not in the long-term. She dropped me off with them when I was six years old."

"I'm sorry, Natalie. I had no idea." He reached across the table and placed his large palm over her hand.

"It's okay. It is what it is."

"That may be so, but it has to hurt not feeling wanted," Jonathan responded.

"It does, but I made my peace with the situation a long time ago. It doesn't affect me like it did when I was growing up being motherless—hell, fatherless, too. But then my grandma and grandpa stepped in and took care of me. For that, I will be forever grateful."

"Sounds like you love them a lot."

"I do," Natalie said with a warm smile. "They're the only parents I've ever known."

"That's how I feel about my grandpa," Jonathan said. "He's ninety-six now and still physically fit, though sometimes he's forgetful of people and places."

"The era he lived through and the stories he tells must be amazing." She loved hearing her grandparents talk about how they first met in the sixties, participating in the Civil Rights Movement and getting married.

"It is. My fondest memories are of riding side by side on our horses as he regaled me with the history of the Lattimore family in the 1900s and our long friendship with the Grandins. But then again, you know about that. You and Chelsea are pretty tight."

"Yes, when we met, we became instant best friends," Natalie said as the waiter arrived with their mouthwatering appetizers. They dug into the meal all while enjoying panoramic views of the Gulf of Mexico.

"Chelsea is good people," Jonathan said, responding to her earlier statement as he munched on calamari. "The whole family is the salt of the earth and have been entwined with mine for years. It's why we were so surprised by the allegations from Heath Thurston. Did you hear?"

"Chelsea mentioned it, but didn't go into detail," Natalie said.

"I appreciate her discretion. Anyway, Heath is claiming he was given oil rights that just so happen to be beneath both the Lattimore and Grandin ranches. Sounds absurd, right?"

Natalie's brow furrowed. "Is there any truth to it?"

"That's what we're trying to find out," Jonathan responded. "We've hired a private investigator to look into the matter and my sister Alexa is representing both families."

"Sounds like you have it under control."

"We do, but needless to say, it has us all up in arms," Jonathan responded. "For me, the ranch is my whole life. I have so much sweat equity in the place, not to mention it's our family legacy. We won't let some outsiders come in and take what's ours, what we've all worked so hard to build."

"Of course not. You're a fair man, Jonathan. It's who I've always known you to be," Natalie replied.

"How can you say that? You hardly know me."

"I know that you'll step in when teenagers are bullying a young girl because she's a few sizes bigger than everyone else." His brow furrowed, so Natalie spilled the story. "You don't remember, do you?"

He shook his head.

"I was thirteen and some boys were making fun of me in the diner. You stepped in and told them they should pick on someone their own size. And if they didn't, they'd have you to deal with."

Jonathan laughed. "Did I really say that? I had mad swag."

Natalie couldn't resist smiling, too. "Oh, don't get full of yourself. I'm merely saying you have integrity, and I haven't met a lot of men like you, Jonathan Lattimore. It takes a special person to step in and help someone else."

"Now you're going to make me blush." When the waiter came back to their table and asked if they wanted dessert, Jonathan looked at her. "What do you say we share the blueberry cheesecake?"

"I'm absolutely on board."

Jonathan was surprised at how easy Natalie was to talk to, but that didn't mean he was ready for anything more after this fling was over. Thus far, she had proven to be an amazing lover and conversationalist, but he liked his life as it was. He only did casual relationships because there was no chance of anyone getting hurt. Rather than talking about the past, he moved to work and shared with Natalie his mother's plan to branch out her culinary business.

"My mother is an amazing cook. We've been telling her for years that she needed to share her recipes with the world, and she did. She got a book deal for a cookbook."

"That's fantastic," Natalie said, beaming across the table at him. "Is she going to do more than cookbooks? I mean, if you look at the celebrity chef market, she can have her own line of cookware, dishes, spices and so much more."

"I know. Alexa told her the same thing, but it wasn't until her agent mentioned it that she's finally listening. Anyway, she's going to be entertaining proposals soon for marketing firms to help with her products."

"If there's anything she needs, let me know. I'd be happy to help."

"Thank you, I appreciate that," Jonathan replied,

and he meant it. "If you're ready, how about a walk?" He patted his stomach. "To walk off some of this meal."

"Sounds lovely."

They took a stroll along the pier past half a dozen restaurants. The pier was alive with nightlife and people milling around. Without consciously thinking about it, Jonathan reached for her hand and laced their fingers together. He heard her suck in a deep breath as she fell in step beside him.

Natalie looked up at him and smiled but didn't say a word. He wondered what she must be thinking with his hot and cold responses. He never envisioned this scenario in his mind when he thought about visiting Galveston. He considered he might meet someone, which is why he bought a pack of condoms. But he and Natalie had already finished the pack.

He'd quickly remedied that situation when he'd gone back to his room. He made a pit stop at the small sundry shop within the resort. Now he couldn't wait to get her back to the room so he could indulge himself in her luscious curves.

Natalie was a surprising but not unwelcome distraction. His life had become rather mundane of late. Work and more work. If he wasn't at the ranch, he was spending time with his family and the Grandins, but lately given the commotion Heath Thurston caused even those gatherings had become rather unpleasant.

And a love life, well, that was nonexistent. It had been years since his divorce from Anne, and Jonathan still had trust issues.

He kept his relationships casual, and it suited him.

There were no misunderstandings or hurt feelings because Jonathan explained from the get-go exactly where he stood on a long-term scenario. He didn't show emotions, so he was better off alone and indulging with a partner when time allowed. This way he'd never let anyone down as he had Anne in their marriage.

He knew everyone in Royal probably thought him some sort of playboy, when that couldn't be further from the truth. He was discriminating about who he went to bed with and often preferred spending time with women outside of Royal, but this thing with Natalie was in his own backyard. Would she be able to handle the end of their fling when it was over?

"What's on your mind?" Natalie asked when they suddenly stopped. Those big brown eyes of hers were staring up at him questioningly.

"I'm wondering if this going to be enough for you," Jonathan answered honestly.

"I thought we agreed to what happens in Galveston, stays here."

"We did."

"But?" Natalie's brow rose a fraction. "You don't believe me?"

"I believe you have feelings for me that you haven't fully sorted out. You don't know me as well as you think you do, and I don't want to lead you on, Natalie. I wouldn't want to hurt you."

Natalie spun away from him to face the dark waters of the Gulf. Anne really had done a number on him. He blamed himself for the demise of his marriage. Jonathan wondered if he could have done things differently. Been more open, been more caring. But he wasn't built that way and he wasn't about to change. He didn't want Natalie to have any illusions that she could change him. He was who he was, and all they would ever have was this vacation fling.

Five

Jonathan hurt Natalie with his lack of faith in her. Natalie was angry that she allowed herself to believe they could have a week together, no strings attached. Swiftly, she began walking away from him back to the resort.

"Natalie, wait!" Jonathan said, catching up to her in a few quick strides.

"Why?" she asked, twirling around to face him. "When you think everything coming out of my mouth is a lie. I can't go back in time, Jonathan, and take back what I said a month ago. I said it. I own it. I've been my authentic self and if you can't trust that, then you're right. This isn't going to work."

She started to move away, but Jonathan caught her arm. "Please don't go."

"Why? You don't trust me." She folded her arms across her chest.

Jonathan sighed audibly. "It's not you, Natalie. I don't trust many people, especially women, but that's about me. Not you."

"Then tell me about it," Natalie asked. "Help me understand."

Jonathan shook his head. "I don't want to talk about it. All I can say is my ex-wife lied to me and did something unforgivable and it's made me leery."

"You don't have to be that way with me."

"I don't want to be," Jonathan responded hotly. "You're a great woman and in case you can't tell, I like you a lot." His fingers drifted into her braids. "And I want to spend this week with you." His bent his head and brought his mouth closer to hers.

Anticipation zinged through Natalie, and she tried to put the worrisome thought out of her mind that Jonathan might not ever be able to trust her or express his feelings, because her entire body craved his kiss. Kisses that were as exciting as each one he bestowed last night. Was that because she had such strong feelings for him? Feelings she was putting on the back burner so she could have this amazing week with him.

Perhaps he was right to be wary of her, but was it so wrong to want a moment in time she would always remember?

His lips brushed hers lightly at first. The initial pressure was soft, but then his lips changed direction as they slid sensuously over hers. He parted her lips so his tongue could delicately probe the inside of her mouth.

Pleasure of the purest kind shot through her in every direction and Natalie couldn't help it—she curled her arms around his neck.

He was hot and hard. She felt his unmistakable desire pressing against her and she surged closer, sizzling with need for him. Jonathan broke the kiss long enough to rasp, "We should get back to the hotel."

Even though she had her doubts about whether she could trust Jonathan with her emotions, she nodded in agreement.

The walk from the pier back to the resort was shorter than Natalie remembered. Could that be because she couldn't wait to get naked with Jonathan again? The disagreement they had was suddenly gone and in its place was a demanding and urgent need for fulfillment.

When she'd been young, being around Jonathan had caused joy to flood through her bloodstream, but now that she was a woman, his impact was more powerful. To know he found her desirable and couldn't wait to get back to the sexual intimacy they shared was disarming. Her mind told her to let the fantasy go and keep a clear head when it came to this man, but her heart said it needed everything Jonathan was offering.

"You feel so good," Jonathan said once they made it back to his room. He slid his arm around her waist and scooped her into full contact with his body. And then his mouth was crashing down on hers, hot and wild. He plundered her mouth, smashing away any barrier Natalie might put between them. He'd fumbled earlier with his words. He wouldn't with his actions now.

Natalie didn't hold back. Her mouth exploded into his again and again and he took it, wanting to taste the very essence of her. His hand burrowed underneath her braids to find the zip at the back of her dress. She was greedy for him as well because her hands dropped between them to tear at the buttons on his shirt. Their clothes soon hit the floor, followed by their shoes. He lifted her off her feet and tossed her onto the bed.

She held her arms open and he joined her, taking her mouth until she was clawing at his back. He lifted his head and saw the gleam of passion in her gaze. He moved his head so he could dip down to her breasts and give them his attention. He lashed them with hot strokes of his tongue and then sucked on her engorged brown nipples until she was grasping his head and moving him exactly where she needed him most.

He eluded her will and tore himself away so he could trail kisses down her stomach and move lower. When his hands came to the moist folds between her legs, his fingers stroked the seam until she purred and opened wider for him. That's when he used his mouth to anoint her with licks and flicks of his tongue until the sweet flood of sensation flowed from her body.

"Jonathan!" A cry ripped from her throat as he lapped her generously. "Please… I need you now."

He surged upward, stopping long enough to rip a foil packet open and sheath himself. Then he was making the entry they both craved. His penetration was deep, and her inner muscles squeezed tightly around him.

Sweet heavens, she made him delirious. He pulled back momentarily and then drove forward again. He repeated the withdrawal and resurgence until she quivered in anticipation; only then did he come in again.

"How does it feel?" he demanded hotly. He wanted to hear, to know she felt as intensely as he did.

"So good…" she moaned underneath him. "So good."

He closed his eyes, expelling a long breath, and then he got caught in the rhythmic union of their bodies. She climaxed first and it seemed to go on and on, but Jonathan didn't stop, not even when he felt her nails on his back. Instead, she urged him toward his own completion and when he finally came, it was so explosive, he let out a roar and she held him against her.

Natalie knew this feeling of bliss couldn't last forever. She and Jonathan had already spent the last couple of days on the beach, in the pool or exploring Galveston. Known for its antique shops, they meandered through them picking up pieces that Natalie wanted for Chelsea's wedding gift. Jonathan discovered she liked taking old pieces and making them fresh again with a little elbow grease or a new coat of paint.

What was most surprising, however, was when she learned Jonathan knew how to play the piano. One night after a four-course meal in one of the resort's high-end restaurants, they went to the piano bar. A pianist was singing and playing a melody of big band classics and pop songs. Natalie couldn't remember how long they stayed, talking and sipping martinis; certainly well past midnight. Eventually, they shut the place down and it was Jonathan and Natalie.

That's when he surprised her by going up to the podium and sitting on the bench to play Beethoven's "Moonlight Sonata." She had no idea he knew how to play or was so gifted. The way his fingers stroked the keyboard and brought her melodic sounds was beautiful. Natalie felt privileged Jonathan allowed her to see another side to him, a softer side. He was always so hard and tough with everyone else, but not with her. He was soft and gentle and tender, but he could be passionate and aggressive when the moment struck.

She joined him on the podium, sitting beside him on the bench. "When did you learn how to play?" she inquired.

"When I was seven years old. My mom was determined that her children learn something cultural and refined other than ranching. She made me learn the piano. My sister Alexa played the violin, while my brother, Jayden, played the saxophone. Eventually, when we adopted Caitlyn, she learned how to play the clarinet."

"Sounds like the Lattimores had quite the band."

"Oh yes," Jonathan laughed. "My dad was amazing on the drums so when the whole family got together, we would make quite the ruckus. I think my mother regretted her decision afterward."

"That's wonderful. I would have loved being part of a big family like yours."

"Was it lonely being the only child?"

Natalie nodded. "My mother was my grandparents' only child, too, so I didn't have any cousins so, yes, it could be lonely at times. Eventually, I learned to embrace the solitude, but tell that to a six-year-old who wants someone to play with."

"Give me your hand," Jonathan ordered.

"Why?"

He didn't wait for her response. Instead, he took Natalie's small hand in his and showed her where to place it on the keyboard, then he walked her through a song, letting his fingers guide hers along the way.

The tune sounded familiar to Natalie. "That's 'Twinkle, Twinkle Little Star.'"

He smirked and tweaked her nose. "How bright you are, Natalie Hastings." Then he leaned over, and his hot, demanding mouth slanted over hers, fusing her with pleasure and firing up all her senses. When the need to breathe forced them apart, he growled, "We should go upstairs."

It didn't take them long to make it back to her suite this time. They quickly divested each other of their clothes and climbed onto her bed, reaching for each other simultaneously. Jonathan cupped her breasts, his thumbs mercilessly teasing the peaks that were desperate for his mouth on them. When he finally sucked one into his mouth, Natalie moaned, her mind fracturing as he grazed his teeth on one nipple. It felt so good to have his mouth on her, but she wanted to do something for him.

She pushed him backward against the pillows and, feeling adventurous, tightened her fist around his virile girth. Heated words spilled from his lips as her hands encircled him, stroking and squeezing until he swelled to life. Then she took his erect length into her mouth and seduced him until he couldn't contain himself and cried out her name.

But Jonathan wasn't a one-sided lover; he hauled her up and she watched him as he slid on a condom with one hand. Then he was setting her astride him until he was buried to the hilt inside her. Then he commanded her, "Ride me."

She did, slowly swaying and gliding on top of him. He grunted and thrust upward to meet her every move. Natalie wasn't sure how many times she called out his name as their bodies became slick with sweat. She only knew that they were on this glorious pleasure ride together hurtling toward a bottomless vortex. When it struck, Natalie cried out her release and Jonathan was right behind her, jerking inside her as they both met the inevitable conclusion.

Natalie knew then that this experience would be one she would remember forever.

Today was going to be one of her favorite memories, Natalie thought two days later. Jonathan had chartered a private yacht for a romantic day getaway for the two of them. She hadn't known what to expect when Jonathan told her to pack her swim gear, lounge attire and something to wear in the evening. She'd been trying not to lick her lips at seeing Jonathan in a tank top that showed off his broad shoulders and the drawstring shorts that revealed his muscular thighs and toned legs.

"Eyes up here." Jonathan jokingly smirked, making Natalie blush because she for sure had been thinking about what she'd like to do later with him.

As each day passed, she was becoming more and more infatuated with Jonathan. He made it clear to her that this week would be all they had. She was terribly disappointed that he couldn't see how great they were together, but she always did her best to curb her feelings so he couldn't see how she wished for more between them. It had been risky for her to move forward with a vacation fling knowing how deep her feelings ran, but at the time it seemed like the only way she could get to know him without an audience. She didn't know how she would be able to walk away when the week was up. Instead, she kept her emotions buried deep. She would analyze them once she was back in Royal.

A limousine picked them up at the resort and whisked them away to Galveston Harbor. A quick ten-minute ride later and they arrived a few yards away from the most beautiful hundred-foot yacht Natalie had ever seen. It was a sprawling two-story masterpiece with an upper balcony.

"Welcome aboard," a white-haired gentleman said, helping her onto the back deck where there was a large outdoor seating area.

"Thank you." Natalie could only imagine he was the captain of the vessel, because he wore an officer's hat with a gold embroidered anchor and wreath, crisp white button-down shirt with an epaulet showing an anchor insignia and four stripes, and black trousers.

"And you must be Mr. Lattimore," he said, lending a hand to Jonathan, who climbed on board with her.

"Yes, sir. Please call me Jonathan."

"The name is Jeff, and I'll be your captain today."

"Pleasure to meet you." Natalie and Jonathan spoke in unison.

"Allow me to show you around the vessel." Jeff walked them through the large open-concept salon and kitchen, which boasted a huge island that currently had a vase filled with roses while rose petals adorned the counter. A bucket of champagne and two flutes stood beside it.

"Jonathan…" Natalie turned to him wistfully, but he shrugged.

"It came with the package," he responded.

So much for letting her get her hopes too high that he held any romantic feelings toward her. She needed to be careful because he was right—she really didn't know him. "I appreciate the effort," she replied as Jeff led them past the powder room downstairs to reveal a spacious bedroom and bathroom at the rear. Eventually, they climbed the stairs to the second floor, which held the balcony. From there, she could see large beanbag chairs on the bow at the front of the yacht.

"This is great. Thank you, Jonathan," Natalie said once the captain left them to their own devices in the salon.

"You're welcome." Jonathan headed to the champagne chilling in an ice bucket and began removing the foil. "Our time is ending soon, and I wanted to make this trip memorable."

He's already thinking about when our affair is ending.

Natalie supposed she shouldn't be surprised. Jonathan was very cut-and-dried about how he felt about continuing a relationship after Galveston. But Natalie wondered how their interactions would be once they were back in Royal. How were they supposed to treat each other? Were they supposed to act indifferent toward each other as if she hadn't known what it was like to have him buried deep inside her?

Natalie wasn't sure she could do that, but if Jonathan didn't want to continue this fling beyond tomorrow, she wouldn't want him to. She wanted a man who *wanted* to be with her. She knew what it was like to feel unloved and unwanted. Her own mother hadn't wanted to keep her.

"Natalie!"

"Hmm…" She realized Jonathan was speaking to her, but she'd zoned out.

"I asked if you would like a glass of champagne."

"I would love some, thanks."

He poured them each a flute. Once she'd sipped hers, Jonathan came from around the bar and wrapped his big strong arms around her waist. She loved it when he did that. It made her feel safe and secure. Too bad it wouldn't last much longer.

"Is there something troubling you?" Jonathan inquired, peering down at her. "You seem distracted."

"Am I?" Natalie feigned a smile. She couldn't very well tell him what she was thinking; he'd run for the hills.

"You are. Did I do something wrong? Is this too much?"

She heard the doubt in his voice. "No, it's just right." She understood their time together had an expiration date, but that didn't mean it didn't hurt that Jonathan wasn't willing to give more than this moment. She couldn't forget that when they were in Royal, he'd avoided her. She would be a fool if she allowed herself to get too attached.

"Good, I wanted you to know how much I've enjoyed spending time with you," Jonathan said. "You've been the greatest surprise, or shall I say revelation, of this forced sabbatical by my parents."

"That's because all work and no play is not very fun, Jonathan." Natalie forced a smile even though her stomach was churning about the end of their fling. "You have to learn to have some sort of work-life balance."

He stared down at her and the sizzle in his eyes made her blood heat and her senses stir. "You're all the balance I need."

Then his mouth covered hers. His warm lips grazed hers seductively and his tongue tantalized with the promise of the all-consuming passion that always surged between them. His kiss was powerful and persuasive as he penetrated her mouth and cleared her mind of negative thoughts.

All she could feel was need. Jonathan understood and hauled her to him, pressing her into his hard arousal. Natalie reveled in the fact that she, a curvy woman, could turn Jonathan's head. He'd steadfastly ignored any of her previous attempts to get him to notice her. Until now. Now she had his undivided attention.

Eventually, it was Jonathan who pulled away first. "Jesus, woman, what are you doing to me?"

"Little ole me?" Natalie asked, touching her chest. "Whatever do you mean?"

"Let's get changed and go swimming," Jonathan suggested. "I think we could both afford to cool off."

"That's probably not a bad idea." Natalie followed Jonathan down the steps to the master bedroom, where he'd placed their bags. While she slipped off her sundress, he used the powder room.

Natalie pulled out a cream-and-black-striped high-waisted bikini she'd been holding out on wearing. She never wore two-pieces because she felt self-conscious about her weight. But she was alone with her lover and there would be no prying eyes except his. So she took the plunge and slipped it on. She put a black crocheted cover-up over it. Grabbing her sunglasses, she exited the bedroom and headed upstairs.

The captain had already pulled away from the harbor and they were now cruising the Gulf. She could see Galveston Island in the distance, but all around them was the ocean.

She found Jonathan lounging on deck bare-chested, wearing swim shorts and sunglasses. His body was breathtaking and Natalie was glad her shades hid her reaction to the electrifying stimulus of seeing him half-naked. He watched her as she approached. Even with his sunglasses she could see his gleaming eyes raking over every inch of her figure until she crossed to the lounger beside his. Suddenly self-conscious, Natalie hesitated to take off the cover-up.

When she glanced at Jonathan he was waiting expectantly. "C'mon, don't be a tease," he murmured. "Take it off."

Sucking in a deep breath, Natalie lifted the cover-up over her head. The hiss that escaped Jonathan's throat made her breath catch, especially when he jerked upright and turned to fully face her.

"You're sexy as hell!"

"You don't have to keep saying that, Jonathan." Especially when she knew it wasn't true. She'd struggled with her weight her whole life and although she was comfortable now in the skin she was in, it was a constant battle.

"Why do you always do that?" Jonathan frowned.

"Do what?"

"Put yourself down. It's not the first time you've done it."

"C'mon, Jonathan." Natalie's sharp burst of laughter surprised Jonathan. "I'm not blind. I know how everyone else sees me."

"And how's that?"

"As the big girl?" Natalie answered. "And I know the in thing right now is about loving yourself no matter your body type, but I've lived with this my whole life. You have no idea what it's like to walk in my shoes and have people snicker behind your back or have boys or men want to date you because they think you're easy."

"Is that what happened to you?"

Natalie shook her head and rose to her feet. She walked over to the rail and looked out over the water. "I don't want to talk about this."

Seconds later, she felt Jonathan behind her. He wrapped his arms around her middle and Natalie leaned back against him, allowing herself a second to imagine that they were more than just lovers and that they were two people in love enjoying a romantic day cruise, but in her gut, she knew it wasn't true. She was on borrowed time.

"I'm sorry you were made to feel that way, Natalie." Jonathan slid his palm around her neck and turned her to face him. "But that doesn't mean that *I* don't find you attractive. You're sexy. Can't you tell? If you leave here with nothing from our fling, know this—you're a beautiful and desirable woman."

"Thank you."

"I didn't say it to you for the accolades. I want you to *believe* it."

"That's easier said than done, Jonathan."

"Then before I leave, I have to some convincing to do and show you exactly what I mean."

That's what Natalie was afraid of: that Jonathan would burrow so deep inside her heart, she would never be able to look at another man, let alone fall in love— and she was already halfway there.

Six

From his chair on the lounge deck, Jonathan watched Natalie on her phone searching Pinterest for ideas on how to modernize the two mid-century modern furniture pieces she found in the antique stores earlier that week. He didn't understand how Natalie couldn't see what he saw. A gorgeous woman who loved seafood, had a penchant for making old things new again and was passionate in bed. He was still trying to figure out how he ended up on a yacht in the middle of the Gulf with a woman he'd tried to steer clear of for years.

But he'd been unable let her leave the bar without him. He'd been eager to test out those full, sensuous lips of hers. She was everything he hadn't known he wanted. He thought the occasional hookup was good enough, but he'd been dead wrong. Natalie awakened his libido like no other woman. He was already thinking of all the places on the yacht where he wanted to make love to her today.

When he told the captain they would need complete privacy, Jeff understood, no questions asked. Maybe he would finally satiate the incorrigible hunger he had for Natalie, because once they got back to Royal, things would change. They had to.

Jonathan refused to have the entire town gossiping about them, especially when he had no intention of putting a ring on her finger. And that's exactly what everyone would expect for a fantastic lady like Natalie. It's what Jonathan wished he could give her, but he'd deadened that side of himself long ago. Marriage, family, children—those were goals and aspirations other people could look forward to, but not him.

He considered his divorce one of his greatest failures. He should never have married so young. He hadn't really known Anne. They'd had a great physical relationship, she came from a good family and he'd thought he was in love, but it had been infatuation. They'd married without his parents' blessing. They'd been sidelined when he and Anne showed up married by a justice of the peace. His mother felt slighted because she hadn't been able to give him a big fat Texas-sized wedding and reception. At least she would get her opportunity with Caitlyn and Alexa, because Jonathan never intended to walk down anyone's aisle. He was done with marriage and relationships altogether, so he couldn't offer Natalie any more than this week. A fling was all he was willing to give.

"Captain Jeff has stopped. Ready for that dip in the ocean?" Jonathan asked, eager to take his mind off the end of their affair and his divorce.

Natalie looked up her phone. "Sure." As she rose to her feet, Jonathan couldn't keep his eyes off her. She was alluring and although she may not like flaunting her curves, she drove him mad. Once they got back to Royal, she would cover her curves in elegant loose-fitting suits.

"Don't you need more sunscreen?" he inquired. He would love to run his hands all over her body.

"Oh yeah." Natalie reached inside the beach bag she had brought upstairs and handed him the bottle. He poured a small amount in his palms and Natalie spun around and pushed her braids forward. The first glide of his hands onto Natalie's silky skin had Jonathan rethinking this scenario, but he couldn't stop now. He applied sunscreen on her shoulders, back and lower until he came to her butt. A peek of her cheeks could be seen in the audacious bikini and Jonathan allowed his hands to roam over them.

"Jonathan…" Natalie damn near purred out his name.

"Hmm…?"

"Are you putting on lotion? Or are you doing something else?"

His body wanted something else, but Jonathan lifted his hands up in surrender. "I was merely making sure you were properly protected."

"Why don't I finish?" Natalie asked and took the bottle from him to apply lotion to her legs. When she was done, she stepped closer to him and slid her hands up his chest. Her eyes flickered up to his. They were both silent. He reached down and traced his finger over her lower lip. She breathed in sharply as he continued moving his finger. She parted her lips and began sucking it into her mouth.

The woman was bewitching him. Suddenly, he pulled away his finger and Natalie had a bereft look on her face, but she didn't say anything. She spun on her heel and to his immense surprise dived off the back of the boat and into the ocean.

He glanced over in time to see her surface in the water. "How is it?"

"Refreshing. You should get in."

Jonathan did because it was exactly what he needed. Otherwise, he would start making love to Natalie and never stop. She made him lose control and it made his head spin. If he wasn't careful, she could strip away all his defenses and make him want to reconsider and extend this fling once they returned to Royal.

As she lay on one of the floats the captain threw out to them, Natalie wished Jonathan could give her his heart as much as he gave her his body. Sometimes she wondered if he was still hung up on his ex-wife. Was that why he refused to commit to another woman? She wanted to find a love like that someday. Find a man who would love her and no other. She supposed that's why it hurt knowing Jonathan would never feel the same way about her.

Natalie wouldn't beg him to reconsider. She had more pride and self-respect than that. So she had to ride this wave until it ended. Once they tired of the ocean, they returned to the boat for the light lunch the captain had catered in for them. Sandwiches, pasta salad and fresh fruit were laid out on the back deck.

"Looks great," Natalie said, patting herself dry with one of the fluffy towels that came with the yacht. Then she sat down and began making a plate. Jonathan did the same and sat across from her. They tucked into the food and crisp white wine in silence. Natalie liked that neither of them felt the need to fill up the quiet moments. With other men, she would be trying to think of something witty to say to keep the conversation going, but with Jonathan she didn't.

Once their bellies were full, Natalie resumed her location on one of the lounge chairs, but not before putting on her large brimmed hat. She was prepared to get deep into a book on her tablet, but Jonathan must have had other ideas because before she could protest, he was pulling her onto his lounger.

"Jonathan, what is—" Those were all the words she got out because he was the aggressor, reaching out to run both his hands through her braids and pull her head down to meet his hungry mouth. He licked and tasted her. Vaguely, she heard herself moan as he put his hands on her hips and pulled her firmly against him. Their lips, teeth and tongues swirled in a delicious mating dance and Natalie barely recognized he'd flipped them over so he was on top.

He reached behind her and untied the knot at the base of her neck, freeing her breasts from their confinement. His hands sought them out, stroking and caressing the tight nipples. Then he lowered his head and feasted on the nearest bud. He alternated between licks, flicks and suction; Natalie closed her eyes as the most exquisite sensations took over her.

His fingers trailed down her leg until he hit the top of her thigh. When he removed her bikini bottom, she parted her legs, allowing his hand into the warm cocoon. "Please…" Natalie would beg for this and only this because that's all Jonathan would give her.

He obeyed her order and slowly began stroking her. Her gasps became louder, so Jonathan accelerated the pace, rotating his thumb around her sensitive nub. She stirred against him, and he increased the pressure until all Natalie could hear was her soft moans and all she could feel was the moisture between her legs.

"That's right, baby. Come for me," he muttered.

Natalie's hips began to buck, and she rotated her pelvis as his fingers drove her wild.

"Jonathan!" When the shudder ripped through her, her inner muscles clamped around his fingers. Her mind blanked completely as sensation after sensation catapulted her into ecstasy. She was still in a haze when she felt the weight of his body settle onto her. He'd already protected them, and her excitement skyrocketed because he thrust inside her in one fell swoop.

When Jonathan began moving in slow, sure strokes, Natalie knew then he would break through any barrier she had put up to prevent herself from falling for him. With each movement, he filled her, becoming one with her, becoming a *part* of her. "Oh yes…"

She arched to meet him, running her nails down

the taut muscles of his back. She kissed his neck, lightly nipping as he liked to do to her, but he still kept the pace. The intensity of his movements as he began pounding into her made Natalie's mind blank. Spasms rocked through her very core, sending her hurtling over the edge, and Jonathan roared as his release crashed around him.

Sometime later, they left the deck to head downstairs to shower together only for Jonathan to wrap her naked body around him once again and press her against the cold tile of the bathroom shower. He departed long enough to roll on a condom before returning so Natalie could tighten her legs around his rock-hard buttocks as he pushed inside her. A groan escaped him as he thrust into her again and again, causing her breasts to push upward. He nipped at their fullness. She screamed, but Jonathan was right there with her exploding all around him.

She fell forward against him like a limp noodle, and he lifted her into his arms and carried her back to the bed. She heard him quietly murmuring her name as she drifted off to sleep.

It took Natalie several minutes to open her eyes and realize she was alone in the bedroom downstairs. She was spent. Natalie knew she should be concerned where this intense lovemaking was leading, but the compulsion to feel everything with Jonathan went beyond sexual gratification. When they were together, they were *making love* and Natalie had to remind herself not to imbue the moment with feelings because Jonathan would never return them.

How could she not when he knew her intimately as no other man had? She was in danger of being seriously in love with this man. She knew he didn't want to hear her feelings and refused to have any of his own. So she kept them to herself, buried along with all the other words she wanted to say, but knew would go unsaid.

Jonathan emerged at the doorway several moments later. "Hello, sleepyhead." His dark eyes were fierce as they regarded her.

"I'm exhausted."

"Too tired for a sunset and dinner?" Jonathan asked. "Captain Jeff called down to tell me the sun is about to set in another fifteen minutes so if we want to catch it, we'd better head up."

"Oh yes, that would be lovely." Naked, Natalie threw back the duvet and rose from the bed. With other lovers, she would have reached for the nearest sheet because she wanted to hide her body, but Jonathan loved every inch of her.

As she walked past him to the bathroom, he smacked her on the rear. "Jonathan!" She spun around.

"What?" He shrugged. "I couldn't resist."

Natalie dressed quickly in a paisley maxi dress with a lightly smocked waist that accentuated her bust. Minutes later, they were climbing upstairs to the balcony where the captain was already looking out over the horizon. He glanced behind him when he heard their footsteps. "C'mon up. You don't want to miss this."

Natalie scurried forward to the railing just as the

sun was setting. Jonathan came up behind her, planting his arms on either side of her, cocooning her in his embrace. Closing her eyes, Natalie wished she could stay here forever with Jonathan.

"Do you always watch the sunset with your eyes closed?" Jonathan asked, glancing down at her closed lids.

Natalie's eyes popped open, and she looked straight ahead, embarrassed at having been caught daydreaming. "Not usually. I was just soaking it all in."

A rumble of laughter escaped from behind her. "It's all right, Natalie," he whispered in her ear. "I'm enjoying the moment, too."

"Do you think Captain Jeff heard us earlier when we were…" Her voice trailed off.

"Making love?" Jonathan offered. "I hope not, but even if he did, I'm sure he knows how to be discreet."

As the minutes ticked by, the vibrant yellow and orange hues of the sun turned to dusky pink and purple. But just as quickly, it was over, as their relationship soon would be.

"I guess that's it, folks," Jeff said. "I've got the makings of your dinner and will go set up, so give me a few minutes and enjoy the view."

"Sounds good, Captain," Jonathan replied as the older man left the balcony. "You're quiet."

"Merely introspective," Natalie responded when she finally hazarded a glance behind her.

"Stay in the moment with me," Jonathan said, sweeping her braids behind her back. "Can you do that?"

"I can try."

"Good." They stayed together like that until the sky turned purple; only then did Jonathan grab her hand. "Let's go eat."

Natalie took his proffered hand, but knew she'd lied to him, because she wouldn't be able to keep her word. She was already thinking about tomorrow and all that it would bring.

Seven

Jonathan awoke the following morning later than normal and instantly knew something was different. Rolling to his side, he glanced to the empty spot where Natalie had lain with him the night before. All that remained was her indentation as well as a note.

He bolted upright as he picked up the slip of paper folded in half. Opening it up, he read:

Jonathan, You have no idea how much I've enjoyed the time we've spent in Galveston. Unfortunately, work beckons. Take care, Natalie.

Take care.

That's it? That's how she was going to leave what could only be described as the best six days of his life? Did she not feel the same? Why hadn't she woken him up so he could have properly told her goodbye?

They'd shared an amazing day on the yacht yesterday. Because if she had, he most certainly would have tried to talk her out of going home. Work be damned! She'd done the right thing, but he had to admit he felt an odd sensation—something like regret because he wouldn't get to enjoy the last day of his trip with her.

Perhaps it was for the best. They had been joined at the hip since they arrived. In and out of each other's beds. And if he had his way, it would have continued until they were due to leave the island. But oh, how he would miss her sweet demeanor, and that gorgeous, sexy of body of hers. They fit together so perfectly. It was like she was *made for him!*

Jonathan had never had a partner who was compatible with him in the bedroom. Natalie left him satisfied and fulfilled each and every time. Whenever they were together, he felt like he couldn't get enough of her. After dinner on the yacht last night, he'd pushed away the plates and had *her* as his dessert.

He smiled at the memory. He'd sat her on the table, hiked up her dress until it bunched at her waist and worked his way lower until he was between her legs. Then he'd spread her wide so he could taste the very heart of her. He used his full tongue to lap her until she was quivering and gripping his head with her hands and crying out his name. Only then did he pull himself up long enough to drop his trousers, slide on a condom and bury himself to the hilt in her. She had felt incredible. Amazing. Glorious.

Throwing back the covers, Jonathan went to the bathroom and turned on the tap as cold as he could take it. He stepped in and hoped it would relieve him of the ache of not having Natalie here to fulfill his fantasies. But worse, he wondered if that wasn't all he craved.

He craved Natalie, the woman who in a short span of time had crept up to fill a void he hadn't known he had. Now what was he supposed to do? He had no room in his life for emotional entanglements because those led to heartache. He made that clear to her, but had he made it clear to himself?

His heart was telling him Natalie was a great girl and perhaps he was doing them an injustice leaving their relationship here in Galveston. But that's what they had agreed to do because he couldn't offer her a commitment or marriage. And if she truly knew him, Natalie would know he was the cold and unfeeling bastard Anne said he was. So he would go back to Royal, and they would go back to the way things were—two people passing in the night.

"Natalie, I appreciate you cutting short your vacation to come back and deal with this. When I texted you an update, I didn't expect you to immediately hop on a plane, but I'm relieved you did," Brent White, her partner, said while he and Natalie looked over the current marketing strategy they had for one of their largest clients, a boutique hotel chain in Houston. The hotel had undergone a multimillion-dollar renovation and was seeking to reinvent itself. H & W Marketing was going to help achieve it.

She and Brent had decided to go into business together after they both worked in corporate America and realized it wasn't for them. It had been an effort of love, but after five years, they were finally making a profit, which allowed Natalie to treat herself to a vacation. It's why this campaign was so important to her and worth cutting her trip to Galveston short.

"Of course. This is my baby," Natalie replied. "We've been working on this marketing campaign for months. I wouldn't want anything to go astray."

"Did you at least enjoy your vacation?" Brent inquired, glancing up at her.

Natalie thought back to yesterday and the way Jonathan had reduced her to moans and gasps on the dinner table, then again on the salon bar and later in bed before they'd eventually made it back to shore. "Yes, I did." She couldn't help the smile that spread across her lips.

"Sounds like someone might not have been alone," Brent stated.

Natalie shook her head. "A girl never kisses and tells."

Brent chuckled. "Your answer told me all I need to know. Let's get back to work."

They worked steadily over the next hours, calling in lunch and dinner while they figured out how they could adjust the campaign now that news had leaked with images of the reno before they were ready.

Marketing had changed dramatically since Natalie first went to school. With social media becoming more and more relevant, she had to stay on the cusp of trends and the best approaches to marketing her clients. She'd even gone back to school and taken a night course on social media to make sure she was on top of her game. In an elite community like Royal, competition was fierce; it's why their firm had gone to neighboring cities like Houston and Dallas to ensure they could stay afloat. She was proud of the progress they'd made.

By the time she drove to her cottage at the end of the night and pulled her oversize Louis Vuitton luggage inside, Natalie was dog-tired. She left her suitcase at the door and kicked off her shoes. Heading to the kitchen, she went to the cabinet and pulled out a wineglass and an opener. When she opened her fridge, she was thankful to see the pinot grigio she kept on hand for such occasions was stocked. After pouring herself a glass, she padded to the living room and plopped down on the sofa.

She'd been so busy for much of the day, she hardly had a chance to check her phone. The one time she had, there had been a text from Chelsea asking her when she was due home so they could catch up.

Little did she know, Natalie thought. She had much to tell her about the week and who she spent it with, but who there wasn't a message from was Jonathan. They had exchanged phone numbers in Galveston so they could reach other, especially when Natalie treated herself to a few hours in the day spa while he went fishing. It came as a surprise to see her phone displayed no notifications that she'd missed a call or text from him.

Really?

Natalie stared down at the phone in her hand. Although they agreed that what happened in Galveston, stayed in Galveston, she expected *something*. Anything. An acknowledgment he received her note. A goodbye. *Hi, how are you? Did you make it back safe to Royal?* But there was nothing. Nada. Apparently, she was under the delusion that she meant more than a warm, willing body next to him. She was wrong.

At least the text from Brent about their marketing campaign gave her an excuse to leave with her dignity. While Jonathan was in a deep, peaceful slumber, she'd written a quick note and placed it on the bed next to him, so he would see it when he woke up. Then she'd sneaked out of his room. She had to. Not just for her business, because Brent probably could have solved this crisis without her.

Deep down, Natalie had run for her own self-preservation. If she hadn't, she would have fallen harder for Jonathan when she was already in too deep. She might have spilled her feelings for him. But not Jonathan. He didn't have any. For him, their fling was finito, over and done with, and she had to think the same. So why did it cut to the quick knowing she meant so little, he couldn't even bother to text or call her? Natalie sighed and sipped her wine.

The last week had changed things between them. Jonathan was no longer an enigma and the hero she crushed on. He was a strong, kind, talented and passionate man who loved to play the piano but also could make her laugh and forget her hang-ups. And when they'd been intimate the passion and connection she and Jonathan shared wasn't like anything else she'd ever experienced. Natalie wished it could have lasted a little bit longer than six days. She would have to put up a brave front the next time she saw him and act like theirs was a meaningless affair. When she knew it was so much more.

Eight

Jonathan was up before dawn. Instead of going into the office to look at figures or research ways to assist Alexa with the oil claim case, he was helping his ranch hands feed and groom the horses and cleaning their hooves while checking for nicks and scratches. Once the horses were tended to, he thought about going up to the main house for breakfast because the smell of his mother's frying bacon always lured him in as well as homemade pancakes, but not today. He'd already eaten at home, fixing himself a quick sausage-and-egg sandwich before filling up his canteen and heading out the door.

He saddled a beautiful Arabian horse named Beauty and after making sure the cinches were tight, stepped into the saddle. Jonathan was going to help his ranch hands find some scattered cows that were on hundreds of miles of open terrain. The fresh air and open fields would give him time to clear his head and get back on track after the week in Galveston. Sometimes cows were like wild animals and began scattering as soon as they saw humans, so he took off galloping so he could herd them back in.

Jonathan desperately needed to get back on track because he'd slept fitfully the night before. Ever since he got back from Galveston two days ago, he felt off. Something was different and he couldn't put his finger on what it was, but everything looked and felt different. The joy he usually got out of being on the ranch was gone and he felt sullen. The exact opposite of how he usually felt. Ranching was in his blood, but not even a hard ride through the acres of Lattimore land could get him out of his slump.

The more he thought about it, the more it occurred to him that he missed Natalie. A sudden memory of her in his bed, looking thoroughly tousled, popped into his head. Then another—of Natalie giving him one of those sweet seductive smiles. Of Natalie looking up at him with her large, trusting brown eyes. Jonathan shook the images from his mind. They had laid out the ground rules of their affair—it would last as long as their vacation, and when it was over, they would go their separate ways. But something about it felt unfinished, as if there was still more to the book and he needed to keep turning the page.

But the truth of the matter was he wasn't looking for a long-term relationship. Ever since his marriage to Anne ended, Jonathan hadn't wanted another foray into the world of heartbreak. He'd learned his lesson and seen what loving someone did. It made you weak and helpless. Made you believe things that weren't true. He had gotten so caught up in the idea of being in love, he never stopped to figure out if Anne truly was the right woman for him.

She checked all the right boxes. Beautiful, smart, came from a well-respected family in the community, but she couldn't be trusted, and he didn't find that out until it was too late. Until she'd done the unthinkable— something they could never recover from. Anne blamed him for causing her to do it, and he resented her for doing it. Divorce papers quickly followed. And so, he retired himself from relationships. It was easier that way.

But…Natalie.

No, he didn't want that for Natalie. She was a good, decent woman. She was so sweet. Trusting. He refused to be the person who hurt her. He would rather remember her lovely face as she slept with her body pressed against his, with warmth and contentment radiating from her every pore. She believed in happy endings, but they weren't for a man like him who couldn't even be bothered to know how unhappy his wife had been. He was too selfish and work-obsessed to see what was happening in his own household. And Jonathan couldn't give her the emotion and vulnerability she craved. He wasn't made that way.

Natalie deserved a man who would love her. Instead of a broken man.

* * *

Natalie was happy for a day off. The last few days had been stressful getting the launch of the hotel back on track, but now that it was, she could take some time for herself doing one of her favorite hobbies on Sunday.

After her hour-long Pilates class, followed by a smoothie and shower, she was on her way to Priceless. The antique store owned by Raina Patterson. The store also served as a studio for people interested in classes like candle making and mosaic design, but Natalie was on the hunt for another piece to go along with the two spectacular finds she'd discovered in Galveston and had shipped home. The entire set would be her wedding gift to Chelsea.

Parking her vehicle, Natalie climbed out and headed toward the large red barn with the white trim. She was perusing an assortment of old tables and bookcases when she stumbled on a beautiful maple slanted-front desk. She was leaning over it and thinking about what she could do to transform it when she heard him.

"See something that catches your eye?" Natalie didn't need to turn around to know the owner of that voice, because he'd been the star of her dreams as well as in person when she'd been in Galveston.

Inhaling deeply, Natalie rose to her feet. "Jonathan." Why did he have to look so damn good in those jeans, a crisp white button-down shirt and his Stetson? She knew the rippled muscular body that lay underneath and her mouth watered.

"Natalie." His eyes were smiling at her, but she wasn't

returning the sentiment. He hadn't bothered to call or text her. "Fancy meeting you here."

"I could say the same. Though I don't recall you mentioning antiquing as a hobby." She made sure her voice was calm, so it belied her inner turmoil at seeing the man she'd become intimately acquainted with in the flesh. After being in each other's company day in and day out, being without him felt like acute torture. And now they were acting as if they were complete strangers. It was frustrating.

"Perhaps it might have grown on me after my time away," he responded with a grin.

After his silence since their return to Royal, Natalie wasn't taking the bait. "Raina has some good pieces. You might find something you like."

"Natalie… I'm not here to purchase anything. I was dropping off a piece of furniture my mother no longer wants."

"Oh, okay then. Well, nice to see you." Natalie started toward the door.

"What about your purchase?"

It could wait for another time as far as Natalie was concerned. She needed to get out of Priceless. Anger and hurt were all rolled into one and she refused to allow him to see how deep her feelings went.

"Natalie, wait!" Jonathan strode behind her and caught up with her outside. "Why does it always feel like I'm chasing after you? Can you just wait a damn second?"

"Why should I, Jonathan?" Natalie hissed, and glanced around to make sure no one was listening. "We are not in Galveston anymore."

His eyes narrowed. "I know that."

Natalie cocked her head to one side. "I suppose you do."

His brows bunched into a frown. "What's that supposed to mean?"

"You know exactly what it means, Jonathan Lattimore. And I have received your message loud and clear." Natalie clicked the remote on her Lexus. "Have a good day." She quickly hopped into the vehicle and turned on the engine.

She wouldn't dare let him see how upset she was—that she felt like rubbish on the bottom of his shoe after he carelessly disregarded what happened between them. She was better off without him.

What the hell just happened? Jonathan stared at Natalie's car revving down the road and away from him. When he'd seen her in Priceless, bending over the desk with her gorgeous ass up in the air, he breathed a sigh of relief. Seeing Natalie again made him want to reignite their affair, see if they could still burn up the sheets.

He could have imagined how intense the attraction was between them in Galveston because of the illicit nature of their temporary arrangement. But on the other hand, his mind was telling him to steer clear of Natalie. She didn't know him well enough to know he rarely showed his emotions or told people how he felt. If she knew, she might rethink the crush she'd had.

Instead, he'd gone for flirtatious, but he must have said something to offend her because she emitted angry vibes. What had he done wrong but honor their arrangement? They hadn't exactly laid the foundation of how they would act toward each other when they were back home in Royal. Maybe if she hadn't rushed away so quickly, they could have figured it out.

But they hadn't.

Instead, he was left with Natalie being mad *at him*.

What had she expected? That he would call and text her like some besotted schoolboy? They were two grown people who *chose* to have a vacation fling. She wasn't about to make him feel guilty as if he'd done something wrong. They had discussed this in Galveston. She said what happened there, stayed there.

She was now acting as if they were an item and he *owed* her something. He only owed her courtesy and respect, which is exactly what he gave her, but he couldn't say the same for Natalie. Had the week in Galveston made her want more from him than he was ready to give?

Given her previous feelings, which the entire town had been able to hear, should he be surprised? Becoming lovers had probably made Natalie hope for more, even though he told her he wasn't looking for a long-term commitment. She must have gotten it in her head that she could change his mind. She couldn't. He was haunted by his disastrous marriage. He blamed himself for not being a better husband. It made him feel unworthy of love.

That didn't mean he didn't want to take Natalie back to his bed. He needed to exorcise her from his mind *and* his body. Only then could Jonathan go back to the solitary life that had become the bedrock of his existence. But as he stared down at the empty road, Jonathan wondered if he and Natalie could really go back to the way they were *before* Galveston.

Natalie called Chelsea on her way home in the car, but her bestie didn't pick up, which meant she was on her own. She wanted to rail at the sky, but she had no one but herself to blame for the predicament in which she found herself in. She'd painted herself into a corner with Jonathan when she agreed their tryst would be limited to their vacation.

At the time, it seemed like the best avenue given how wary Jonathan had been after the first time they made love. Secretly, she'd been thrilled to know that the man she crushed on for ages found her attractive. She suggested a vacation fling knowing it was the *only* way she could keep Jonathan in her bed, but it backfired. Because although she may not have been expecting a Hollywood movie ending where Jonathan suddenly realized she was the woman he'd been waiting his whole life for, she certainly thought he'd at least call or text her.

When neither of those things happened, Natalie realized how delusional she'd been. Jonathan was only with her for sex and companionship and now that the vacation was over, so were they. It hurt so much seeing him today and knowing how good they were together and having him want nothing more to do with her. No, correction, she'd seen the hungry look in his eye when she'd spun around to face him, so she could only imagine he wanted another roll in the hay for old times' sake.

Well, she wasn't going to do that again. She had to at least demand a relationship. Sex for sex's sake was no longer on the table. She was done doing things his way. She wasn't going to apologize for wanting more.

Nine

Jonathan and his younger siblings, Jayden, Alexa and Caitlyn, gathered at their family home later that afternoon. It wasn't unusual for the entire family to be in one place. There was nothing his mother loved more than having all her children present so she could be in full mother hen mode.

One of the big reasons she was thrilled was because Alexa had come home *permanently*. Originally, his sister had visited for Victor Grandin Sr.'s funeral, but after Layla Grandin asked Alexa to stay on and help with Heath Thurston's claim, she had remained in town. That's when she met and fell in love with her former school rival, Jackson Strom. Now she and the CEO of the PR firm were head over heels in love and engaged to be married. Jonathan couldn't believe that *both* his sisters had been struck by Cupid's arrow. He refused to go down that road again. He would be happy with his casual affairs.

I wonder what Natalie is doing?

Dammit, he had to stop obsessing about Natalie and instead focus on enjoying family time.

After everyone dispersed, Jonathan stayed behind because he wanted to talk to his mother. He'd been mulling this over in his mind since his return and he was certain he was doing the right thing.

"Jonathan, I thought you'd gone," his mother said when she came into the kitchen and found him raiding the cookie jar. Like him, she liked an evening treat and he'd banked on the fact that she would grab a snack before she and his father headed upstairs to bed.

"You know I can't resist your oatmeal chocolate chip cookies."

She beamed with pride. "No one knows the secret to making chocolate chip cookies taste amazing is the extra bit of oatmeal." She went to the commercial-sized fridge and pulled out a jug of milk. She poured herself and Jonathan a glass.

"But something tells me that's not the only reason you're here," she said, handing him his glass.

"Thanks." He took a large gulp of milk, uncaring he had a milk mustache. "And no, it's not."

"What's on your mind?" She reached over and with her thumb wiped away the milk.

"I wanted to know if you've selected a marketing firm to help take your culinary products to the public."

Despite the chilly reception Natalie gave him earlier, he still believed in her talent.

His mother shook his head. "No, not yet. I'm still entertaining offers."

"Could I be bold and make a suggestion?"

"I'm all ears."

"Natalie Hastings. She and her business partner own a marketing firm here in Royal," Jonathan said. He glanced in his mother's direction, but her expression remained neutral. "If you're looking for a local firm, I don't think you can do any better than Natalie's company."

His mother tilted her head to one side and her dark brown eyes pierced his. "Is that so?"

"You sound doubtful."

"Not of Natalie's firm. I've heard of them, and I'd be happy to entertain a proposal. I'm more curious about why you're making the recommendation."

"I don't follow."

"C'mon, Jonathan," his mother said, chuckling, and he could see he wasn't fooling her for a second. She was on to him. "Don't act dense. If you recall, the entire family was there last month at the Texas Cattleman's party. We heard Natalie's declaration and know you're the object of her affection. And suddenly you think she's the best thing since sliced bread. What gives?"

Damn. His mother wasn't going to let him off the hook easily. He had to give her something. Throw her a bone. "I recently got to know her and found her to be a charming and talented woman."

His mother smiled at that statement. "That's high

praise coming from you, considering you haven't brought a woman home to meet the family since Anne."

Jonathan rolled his eyes upward. That name was persona non grata in this house. "Please don't bring up my ex."

"With pleasure. She's one of my least favorite people," his mother replied. "And I'll give your Natalie an audience, but she'd better bring it. I don't give out handouts."

He doubted she was "his Natalie" anymore. The lady was mighty upset with him. "Thanks, Mom." Jonathan strolled over to her and, grasping her by the shoulders, kissed both her cheeks. "I appreciate it."

Jonathan quickly exited the kitchen before his mother could pepper him with more questions about how and *when* he'd gotten to know Natalie. Because he knew he hadn't fooled her for a second. She knew something was afoot and she would use her powers of persuasion and the rumor mill of Royal to find out the truth. Lucky for him no one knew he and Natalie had become lovers and that's exactly the way he intended to keep it.

"Natalie, baby girl, it's so good to see you," her grandmother said when Natalie stopped by her childhood home to check on her grandparents that evening. They'd raised Natalie after she was dropped off *unwanted* by her biological mother.

"Hey, Mimi," Natalie said, using the affectionate name she'd given her at two years old. She kissed her cheek as she stepped inside the three-bedroom home located in the center of Royal. "I brought you over a caramel cake from the diner."

"Thank you, sweetie. You didn't need to do that."

"It's no bother. I thought it would go great with whatever you were cooking up for Sunday dinner."

"I made the usual, some baked chicken, fried cabbage and some corn bread. You hungry?"

"If that's what's for dinner, then that's an absolute yes. Where's Granddaddy?" Natalie dropped her purse and glanced around the room.

"Oh, he went over to help give the neighbor a jump. He'll be along shortly. Come on in and sit for a spell. We can catch up about your trip to Galveston. Was it the getaway you needed after the hoopla of the last month?"

Natalie chucked inwardly. How could she forget professing her adoration for Jonathan live in front of the entire town? It all seemed like a moot point now, given they'd become lovers. He may not have been into her before, but he hadn't been able to get enough of her during their vacation.

"Yes, Mimi, it was exactly what I needed to put the past behind me," Natalie responded. Maybe that would be all the closure she would get. For a brief moment, she got to have her heart's desire, and now she knew Jonathan was bad for her.

"That's good. Because I wouldn't want you to get hurt and think the Lattimore boy would be interested in you when he's never approached you."

Ouch. Is that how everyone saw her? As some desperate female?

"It's over now. I'm moving on."

"So, you're willing to date someone else?" her grandmother asked. "If so, I know a great young man from church who's been dying to go out on a date with you."

"No, thanks, Mimi. Really, if you don't mind, I'd like to focus on my business."

"You're not getting any younger, my sweet. If you want a family someday, you can't wait around. It's not so easy for women to get pregnant these days. You have to take the bull by the horns if you want to meet a good man."

Natalie chuckled. "I do want a family and kids, but it doesn't have to be right now. H & W Marketing is doing so well now. We can't lose momentum."

"All right. Well, you can't blame a mother for trying, can you?"

Natalie grinned broadly from ear to ear. He grandmother didn't often refer to herself as Natalie's mother, so it was great to hear because Natalie felt the same way. Claudette and Carlton Hastings were her parents, and she loved them.

Seconds later, the back door opened and her grandfather walked in. "Baby girl!" He swept Natalie into his arms and any negative thoughts she had instantly melted away in the safety of his arms. He'd always had that effect on her. Even when she was a little girl, there was nothing her daddy couldn't do.

"Hey Pop-pop," Natalie said when he finally placed her back on her feet.

"I didn't know you were stopping by."

"Spur-of-the-moment thing," Natalie replied.

"She brought one of the diner's famous caramel cakes."

Her grandfather rubbed his belly. "It's going to taste great after the meal you prepared, sweetheart." He rushed over to give his wife a quick peck on the lips. "Are you staying for dinner, Nat?"

"Yes, sir."

Natalie wouldn't miss this for the world. A chance to be with her family, with people who truly cared for her. Her mimi was right. She had to stop wishing things might be different with Jonathan, because they weren't. He made his intentions clear when he didn't contact her. Whatever they might have shared was over. She was moving forward with her life and if that didn't include Jonathan Lattimore, so be it. She refused to be his booty call.

Ten

"You won't believe this," Brent said when Natalie came into H & W Marketing the next morning and he stopped by her office. "Guess who is publishing a cookbook and looking for a marketing firm to help with the launch of a corresponding product line?"

"Who?"

"Barbara Lattimore."

"Really?" Natalie fiddled with papers on her desk and tried to act like she had no idea, but Jonathan had mentioned his mother was branching out into culinary products.

"She asked to meet with us," Brent replied enthusiastically. "She's sent out a request for proposal, but apparently she's already found a publisher for her new cookbook and her agent indicated she wants to get into spices and homemade baking mixes. I'm told eventually this could lead to cookware and bakeware."

It was fantastic news and normally Natalie would be excited, but it could potentially put her in Jonathan's orbit and after their last foray at Priceless, she wasn't keen on a repeat performance.

Brent frowned. "Why aren't you more excited?"

"You do remember I was outed in front of the entire town for having a crush on her son?" Natalie replied. "Or did you forget?" She had never revealed to Brent *who* she had a tryst with while on vacation.

"Of course I haven't. But this is business. We can't let emotions get involved. Snagging a campaign like this in its infancy stages could put us on the map."

Natalie took a deep breath and tried to be more excited. "I'm sorry if I'm being a Debbie Downer. I don't mean to be. This is great! And yes, we will absolutely put together a proposal for Mrs. Lattimore—one that will knock her socks off."

Brent touched her nose. "There's my girl. I need your fighting spirit on this one. And who knows, this could be exactly what the older Lattimore son needs to finally get off his horse and ask you out."

If he only knew, Natalie thought as he left her office. She and Jonathan shared a connection in Galveston, but did she really know him? A relationship took time, and they'd only been together less than a week. There was probably a lot about him she didn't know. At times, her heart wanted to know what secrets and hurts lay hidden beneath the real reason Jonathan preferred casual hookups, but her mind warned her to protect herself. And instead find a man ready for love.

Later, after they worked on the RFP, Natalie left the office for the Texas Cattleman's Club. She was meeting Chelsea there for lunch. While she drove, she tried not to think about what having Barbara Lattimore as a client would mean.

Surely, if she was at the main house working with Jonathan's mother, she would hardly see her son? If she recalled, Jonathan handled the ranch's administrative functions as well as operational duties with his brother, Jayden, which kept him plenty busy.

Natalie had only met Barbara Lattimore a few times in passing. She was warm, bubbly and never met a stranger; she easily conversed with everyone.

When Natalie arrived at the club, she stopped at the valet and handed him her keys while she went in to meet her best friend.

She was waiting at the hostess station when she saw Jonathan exiting the restaurant with another man. They shook hands and the other gentleman departed. At first, she was considering not speaking because he seemed deep in thought, but then again, she would have to get used to facing Jonathan in public situations even though her heart rate ratcheted up a notch when they were in close proximity. "Jonathan."

He glanced up when he saw her and blinked several times. "Natalie?" He looked surprised to see her. It was as if she was suddenly invisible to him again as she'd once been. How was that possible after everything they shared?

"Is everything okay?" she asked instead. She hadn't seen him since Priceless, but she'd cooled down since then. Natalie refused to be one of those women who couldn't take a hint after a hookup was over. She understood the rules of their fling, but that didn't mean it didn't hurt. She wasn't made of stone.

"Everything is fine. Just a lot going on right now." He lowered his head and instead of looking at her, his eyes shifted restlessly back and forth.

"Anything I can do to help? I'm a pretty good listener."

He shook his head. "No, but thank you. It's a family matter."

Natalie nodded curtly. "Of course. Didn't mean to overstep. If you'll excuse me." She headed straight for the exit. If she stayed another minute and watched Jonathan act as if nothing ever happened between them, she was going to scream.

Every time they saw each other, the situation was becoming more and more awkward. She wanted to tell Jonathan he had nothing to fear from her, but the keep-away vibes he gave resonated. And she would do just that. Natalie was done wishing and hoping the situation would get better between them.

"Hey, where are you?" Natalie asked after dialing Chelsea's number once she was in her vehicle.

"Sorry! I'm just leaving now. I'm running late. I was preoccupied with Nolan."

"It's okay. You're newly engaged. How about I come there instead after work?"

"That would be perfect. Come on over. I miss you.

We are overdue for some girl talk, and it's easier to talk here than at the TCC anyway."

"I hope you have some liquor, because I might need the hard stuff."

"Only beer. Can you pick up some on your way over?"

"I'll buy a big bottle and see you this evening."

Natalie ended the call. She had been holding this inside for far too long. She hoped that by finally sharing her feelings with Chelsea, she could figure out how to get past making the biggest mistake of her life by becoming intimate with Jonathan.

Damn.

He'd blown it again, Jonathan thought, watching Natalie drive off. He hadn't been able to get the risk his family was facing out of his head. Despite his grandfather's failing memory, Jonathan suspected he knew more than he was letting on. It's why he arranged to meet with the private investigator Jonas Shaw himself and go over the details. It wasn't that he didn't trust Alexa, but every rock had to be overturned to ensure their family legacy would be preserved. Jonathan had worked too hard, given up too much of himself to the land, to let an outsider come in and take his inheritance.

But he hadn't meant to be dismissive with Natalie. He was distracted by what was going on with his family. Was he using it as an excuse not to think about Natalie and all they shared? Hell yes! He hadn't been able to get the curvy vixen out of his mind. Usually, after

...imate with a woman, he turned
...work, to the ranch he loved, but with
...made him *feel* things—happiness at see-
...ce each morning when he woke up, relaxed
...he was with her and excited at sharing a bed with
...r each night.

And he didn't like it. Jonathan preferred not feeling anything because he knew how to handle that existence, but these emotions were too much. He didn't
know how to deal with them. And he certainly couldn't
give Natalie the relationship he knew she wanted.

It's why Jonathan asked his brother, Jayden, over to
his house later that evening. Maybe talking things out
would help bring him some clarity.

"Bro!" Jayden slapped his back when he came into
Jonathan's. "Not that I don't appreciate the invite, but
what's going on? You sounded stressed on the phone."

"I've got a bit of female trouble." As they passed
by the foyer, Jonathan glanced at his piano. Usually
playing helped, but it had done little to alleviate the
insomnia he'd been dealing with since returning from
his vacation.

"That's what brothers are for," Jayden responded,
following him into his oversize living room.

"Thanks, Jayden. I appreciate it. I've had a lot on my
mind lately. I was hoping I could bounce it off you."
Jonathan flopped onto the sofa in front of the ninety-
inch high-definition flat-screen television.

"Sure, but I admit I'm surprised," Jayden replied,
sitting in the armchair across from him. "You've always kept your feelings to yourself. You're a hard shell

to crack for your family. I can only imagine how s.
one else might receive you."

"Thanks a lot." Jonathan frowned.

"Listen, don't be mad, but I speak the truth. You
can be a little bit of a brick wall."

Jonathan snorted. "Tell me how you really feel."

Jayden laughed. "That's exactly what I'm doing.
Listen, we can go back and forth like this for hours.
Why don't you take it from the top and tell me what
happened?"

"I slept with Natalie."

"Whoa!" Jayden sat forward in the chair. "I wasn't
prepared for that confession, but just so I'm clear, is this
the same Natalie who announced to all of Royal she
had a huge crush on you and thought you were—" he
put his hand up in air quotations "—the most amazing
man she'd ever met? You mean that Natalie?"

"Yes."

His brother was silent for several minutes and
rubbed his chin. "When did this happen? I don't recall seeing the two of you around town recently. Otherwise, the gossip mills would be on fire right now and
Mom would be hearing wedding bells."

Jonathan shook his head adamantly. "No, I'm not ever
getting married again." He wasn't cut out for relationships or commitment. He didn't deserve a happy ending.

"You say that now, Jonathan, but you may not mean
that a couple of years from now," Jayden replied. "You
got married young before you really knew each other.
You didn't do your due diligence."

"You don't need to tell me that," Jonathan replied.

"And is that how you feel about sleeping with Natalie?" Jayden asked. "Because you shouldn't beat yourself up. We've all had one-night stands, though you've yet to tell me any details including how you were able to keep this quiet without it getting back to the family."

"Because it wasn't one night, and it didn't happen in Royal."

Jayden used his fingers to reach up and scratch his head. "Excuse me? You told me you slept with Natalie."

"Yeah, but I never said it was just once, you made an assumption."

"Which you didn't correct," Jayden replied. "What's going on, Jonathan?"

"It's exactly as I've said. Natalie and I hooked up. It happened more than once. Hell, it happened often while I was in Galveston. And I have to tell you, Jayden, it's the best sex I've ever had in my life."

"Get out!"

"She blew my mind, bro. Maybe because the chemistry between us was so unexpected. I didn't go there looking for anything. I was annoyed because Dad and Mom made me go on vacation, but then on the first night, I saw Natalie and…well, we became lovers. And it was so damn good."

"So you had a vacation fling with Natalie?"

"Bingo. Give this cowboy a cowboy hat." Jonathan smirked. "We had an incredibly hot and passionate fling. It's like she's got me punch-drunk and I can't seem to clear my head of her, of her gorgeous body and everything she can do with it."

Jayden put a hand up in the air. "Enough with the

visuals, please. We know each other and I don't want to think about Natalie getting busy with my brother."

"I'm sorry, but it's how I feel," Jonathan replied, jumping up and starting to pace his hardwood floors. "She's in my head and I can't get her out."

"Have you ever thought that maybe she shouldn't come out?" Jayden responded. "You've been living like a monk for years. Maybe it's time you let the *player* come out to play."

"That's crude, Jayden."

"But true. All this has done is show you that you can't cut yourself off from the world. You have to let someone in at some point, Jonathan. You have needs."

Jayden's words sounded familiar. Natalie had told him that everybody needed someone, but he chose not to focus on that. He said instead, "Yes, I have needs."

"But since Anne, you've been closed off. Afraid to take a chance."

Jayden was right, but Jonathan refused to tell him so; he wouldn't give his baby brother that much vindication.

"I'm happy Natalie took a chance on you. How did you guys meet up?"

Jonathan filled Jayden in on their first encounter at the resort and how after that night Jonathan considered walking away, but once Natalie indicated she was open to a vacation fling, they carried on a passionate affair.

"The whole time?" Jayden inquired.

"Yeah. A little under a week, but she was called back to work unexpectedly."

"Do you feel shortchanged because you two didn't have the full week to explore each other?"

"No, not per se."

"Then what? Spit it out, Jonathan, I'm getting older by the minute."

Jonathan chuckled. "I miss her and not just in bed. I miss her smile. Her warmth. She's all heart, ya know? And so much more than I bargained for."

"Then maybe you should see where things go between you?"

Jonathan shook his head. "Nah, man. *We* are not going anywhere. I told you, I've been down that road before and if you don't remember, it ended in disaster."

"That may be so, but not every woman is like Anne. You can't generalize. You already said Natalie is special, and she must be because it's the first time in nearly a decade I've heard you talk like this about a woman."

Jonathan refused to give anyone that kind of power over him. Anne had him in knots. She might have been beautiful but she was utterly needy and no matter what he did to try to show her he cared, it produced the opposite result. Jonathan aspired to do things well—he supposed that was the curse of being born the eldest— and failure hadn't been an option.

He'd been devastated by the demise of his marriage and felt to blame because Anne complained he wasn't there for her or was always working on the ranch. Jonathan wanted a woman who was independent who didn't need him like Anne did.

Natalie was definitely the antithesis of Anne. She was not only beautiful, but she was strong and independent. He loved listening to her ideas for H & W Marketing, the firm she started with her best friend. In fact, even though he sensed she was angry with him, she didn't stay and cry or pout like Anne would have done. Instead, she kept it moving. He appreciated that. Respected it.

"I think you're doing yourself a disservice," Jayden replied. "If Natalie is all that, you should be trying to snatch her up before another fella comes along and realizes what a prize she is. Then you'll be the one with regrets."

"I don't know, Jayden." He wasn't sure he could reciprocate her feelings.

"You would rather stay single?" Jayden inquired. "Because who knows, you could be rejecting your future wife."

Jonathan shook his head. "I'd rather stay single forever than experience the highs and lows I had with Anne. I can't do that again."

"You're willing to forgo all you and Natalie could be because you're afraid?"

"I'm not afraid. I'm practical. Trust me, I've thought about this long and hard. There may be some residual attraction left between me and Natalie, but in time it will fade. Just like her feelings if she ever got the chance to really know me."

Jayden shrugged. "All right. I don't know why I'm here if you've already made up your mind. But don't say I didn't warn you."

"I'm so mad at myself," Natalie said to Chelsea. After work, Natalie had shown up at Chelsea's with a bottle of Jose Cuervo and margarita mix and a bag of limes. And once she got all the ingredients into Chelsea's Ninja and pulsed, the drinks were flowing, and Natalie was spilling her guts.

"I can't believe you kept this juicy news to yourself this entire time." Chelsea shook her head with disbelief. "You're usually not good at keeping secrets, and about Jonathan of all people?"

Natalie took a huge gulp of her margarita. "I wanted to tell you, but you've been so busy with Nolan being happy in love. I didn't want to bring my misery to you."

"We're besties," Chelsea said. "You can call me anytime. My door is always open. Even once Nolan and I are married, that won't change."

Natalie glanced down at the beautiful diamond ring Chelsea was sporting. "You're so lucky to have found someone who loves and wants to be with you. I want that someday."

"And you will find it, too," Chelsea replied, reaching across the sofa to squeeze her hand. "I truly believe there's someone for everyone."

"I thought that someone was Jonathan."

"You've always had a soft spot for him," Chelsea responded, sipping her drink. "I'm not surprised that when the opportunity presented itself you went for it."

"It was so passionate. So intense." Natalie's eyes grew large with excitement at remembering how hot the sex was. "I didn't know I could feel that way."

"With the right person, sex can be transformative. Who brought up the idea of having an affair?" Chelsea inquired.

Natalie raised her hand. "That was my bright idea,

but you have to understand the circumstances. We had just slept together and the next morning, the attraction was still simmering on the surface. I wanted to act on it, but I could tell Jonathan was afraid and ready to run, so I clutched on to the first life vest I could find and said what happened in Galveston, stayed in Galveston."

"You were giving him an out at the end?"

Natalie nodded and hung her head low. "I didn't want it to end, and I feared he would walk away, but maybe I should have let him. It would have been a one-night stand that we remembered fondly. Instead, I let myself get in too deep. We became lovers and I stayed in his bed night after night."

"And you fell harder for him, didn't you?" Chelsea asked over the rim of her margarita glass.

"I did, so when Brent texted about issues with the hotel campaign, I used it as a way out to save face so Jonathan wouldn't see how hard it was for me to walk away. But I...I never imagined he wouldn't at least call or text me when I got back. If nothing else than to know I made it back safely, but nothing. It was like I was out of sight, out of mind. This isn't some crush anymore. I got to know him, share our common interests, become lovers. I have feelings for him, and it hurts to feel rejected."

"Of course it does, because you want him to share your feelings."

"But he doesn't."

"You don't know that. He stayed with you for six days in Galveston," Chelsea responded. "It tells me you meant something to him."

"Then why has he been silent?"

"Because he doesn't know how to proceed from here. He's trying to respect your wishes. Despite his protests to the contrary, Jonathan likes you. You should capitalize on that. Pursue him. You might be surprised on how things turn out."

Natalie shook her head. "No, I couldn't do that." She couldn't put herself out there like that. What if he rejected her?

"I've known Jonathan my whole life. He's a good man who went through some hardships in his first marriage, but it's possible he could change. I mean, look at me and Nolan. The odds were against us from being together with his brother going after my family, but we thrived despite the odds against us. I think you can, too. You have to be willing to take a risk to try to break through the walls Jonathan has erected."

Chelsea had a point. She had given herself a pep talk that she was going to take control of her life. The best way to do that was to go after what she wanted. And Jonathan was *who* she wanted. Who she'd always wanted, not just for a weeklong fling, but for a lifetime. "Okay, I'm going to do it."

"You are?"

"You sound surprised."

Chelsea shrugged. "I shouldn't be. I've never seen you talk this way about another man because none of them have ever measured up against Jonathan, the man you've used as the yardstick for all the others."

"You're right," Natalie acknowledged. Her schoolgirl crush for Jonathan was over. In its place were the feelings of a grown woman who knew what it was like to be in the arms of her lover. A lover she would have to pursue until he could see the potential she'd always known—which is that they were meant to be.

Eleven

The next couple of days went by slowly for Natalie. She couldn't get Chelsea's advice out of her head. Natalie was trying to figure out the best approach. Or maybe honesty was the right one. She should come out and tell Jonathan that she wanted him, but not to be friends with benefits. She had to make it clear that she wanted a relationship that led to a long-term commitment. But what would he say? It was risky and went against her self-protective instinct to walk away.

Jonathan had ample time to come to her and let her know he wanted to rekindle their affair, but he hadn't. Instead, he'd given her mixed signals, being flirty at Priceless and distant at the Texas Cattleman's Club. It was hard to read him or know what he wanted.

Rather than a full-on pursuit, she chose instead to

go to the Lattimore ranch after receiving an invitation from Barbara Lattimore. Mrs. Lattimore had reviewed H & W Marketing's proposal and wanted to speak with them. However, this morning Brent had come down with a stomach bug, so Natalie was going solo to the meeting. Natalie didn't know if she would seek Jonathan out afterward. She would decide once she made it there. Just in case she ran into him, Natalie wore her favorite dress. A geometric-and-chain-print dress with a trumpet sleeve. The belt around her waist helped show off her curvy figure.

An hour later, she pulled her Lexus through the gates of the Lattimore ranch. She'd never been here before. She'd been to the Grandins' ranch many times with Chelsea. It had been Chelsea's father who convinced Natalie to try horseback riding. She'd been wary of entrusting her safety to the large animals and certainly hadn't thought with her weight she could get on one, but Mr. Grandin assured her she was in good hands. And now Natalie considered herself a competent rider. She wouldn't win any competitions, but she knew how to handle a horse.

She parked her car outside the beautiful two-story home with a brick facade and made her way up the steps to ring the doorbell. Several seconds later, a woman who had Jonathan's honey-brown complexion and warm smile opened the door to greet her. Barbara had on jeans, a stylish tunic with beading around the V-neck and cowboy boots.

"You must be Natalie," Barbara Lattimore said.

"I am, and you're Mrs. Lattimore?"

"The one and only. Please come in." She motioned Natalie toward a sitting room right off the foyer. "Would you like some sweet tea or lemonade?"

"I would love both if you don't mind," Natalie replied. "I love a good Arnold Palmer."

"Coming right up, and please call me Barbara."

"Thank you, Barbara." While Barbara left to fetch the drinks, Natalie moved over to the sitting room's wood mantel that held several images of the family.

Natalie easily found Jonathan in the family photos. She was admiring them when Barbara returned with a tray carrying a pitcher of iced tea and lemonade and placed it on the coffee table.

"You have a beautiful family, Barbara."

Barbara smiled and poured equal amounts of each pitcher into a glass for Natalie and handed it to her. "Hopefully that's to your liking."

Natalie took a sip. "It's delicious. Thank you. Though I have to admit I was surprised to receive the invitation to meet with you."

Barbara angled her head to one side. "Really? Jonathan spoke very highly of you and your firm."

"He did?" Natalie chucked nervously and sipped her drink. She hadn't expected he would do anything for her given they weren't on speaking terms. "I mean, he mentioned your cookbook and new products but didn't give me any indication he recommended me."

Barbara shrugged. "That's Jonathan for you. Of all my children, he's always been the hardest to decipher his feelings. He keeps them close to the chest, but not you, my dear."

"What?" Natalie nearly spit out her drink and began coughing instead.

"My apologies for being blunt." Barbara handed Natalie a napkin from the tray, which Natalie used to quickly wipe her mouth. "It's one of my many flaws. Unlike my son, I don't like to beat around the bush."

"Ma'am?"

"At the Texas Cattleman's party, I believe you gushed about how amazing my son was."

Ohmigod, Natalie was mortified. If she could, she would wrinkle her nose or snap her fingers to transport herself out of the room, but instead there was no way out. She glanced up and met Barbara's gaze head-on. "Uh, yes, yes, I did."

"It was nice to hear someone was so fond of him given his rather solitary lifestyle these past years. It gave me hope that maybe he would get out of the rut he's been in and meet a nice young lady like yourself who so clearly adored him, but then weeks went by and nothing. I thought all was lost."

Natalie didn't know where Mrs. Lattimore was going with this line of conversation, so she remained mum and Jonathan's mother continued.

"Imagine my surprise when he spoke so highly of you. Indicated you'd spent some time together. That's when my mom radar went off and I couldn't resist picking up the phone to contact you. Lucky for me your partner, Brent, answered. A wonderful young man."

"I think so."

"Indeed." Barbara smiled conspiratorially at Natalie, and she wondered what his mother knew that she didn't. She soon found out. "Brent told me about your business, how you were thriving and making a profit, so much so, you had just gotten back from a vacation in Galveston."

Natalie swallowed the lump in her throat.

"Did you know my husband and I sent Jonathan to that very city for a weeklong getaway?"

"That was very generous of you." Natalie's throat felt as dry as sandpaper.

"Yes, it was. Small world, isn't it? That you and my son would be in the same city, at the same resort, at the exact same time?"

"Did you arrange for Jonathan to be there?" Natalie inquired.

His mother shrugged. "I may have overheard Chelsea Lattimore saying you were going to a fantastic resort in Galveston and seeing as how you adored my son, I thought he might need a kick in the right direction."

"Barbara…" Natalie couldn't believe her ears. His mother was playing matchmaker.

"Jonathan has been so lonesome all these years. He needs a fine woman to spend time with."

"Things didn't quite go as you envisioned. We aren't together."

"Not yet." She responded with a smile and Natalie wondered what else Mrs. Lattimore had in store. It appeared nothing, because Barbara began discussing her next goals for her culinary empire and soon, they were talking marketing strategies.

They were so engrossed nearly an hour later that Natalie didn't hear the front door open until she glanced up to see Jonathan's towering figure standing in the sitting room doorway. He looked sexy in a designer navy suit with a gray tie that looked like it cost more than she made in a month. Natalie didn't recall ever seeing him in business attire. He definitely wore the suit well, as it was molded to his chiseled frame. "Natalie? What are you doing here?"

"Jonathan Lattimore! Is that any way to treat a guest in our home?" his mother admonished.

Properly chastened, Jonathan lowered his head. "I'm sorry, Mom. I was just surprised."

"*I* invited Natalie over to discuss my expansion plans for my culinary business. You did recommend her firm," his mother stated.

At the comment, Jonathan's dark brown eyes pierced Natalie's waiting for her reaction, but she didn't have one. She was thoroughly disconcerted by the entire meeting. First, learning Jonathan recommended her and his mother's matchmaking by sending Jonathan to her Galveston resort.

"Well, I should be going." Natalie rose to her feet and began shuffling papers back into her shoulder briefcase. "It was lovely to have met you, Barbara. I truly hope I've shown you that H & W Marketing is the right firm to represent you on this journey."

"Of that, I have no doubt," Barbara responded, and walked over to shake Natalie's hand. "You're hired."

"I am!" Natalie couldn't contain the glee from her voice. She never expected Mrs. Lattimore would actually hire her firm.

Barbara nodded. "Send over your contract and I'll have my attorney look it over."

"Yes, ma'am!"

"Jonathan, do be a dear and walk Natalie out," his mother said. "I have to attend to dinner."

"Of course." His eyes never left Natalie's. "It would be my pleasure."

Once his mother left the room, Natalie didn't know what to do. She wanted to take Chelsea's advice and let Jonathan know what she wanted, but they were in his parents' home and now wasn't the right time.

Natalie reached for her briefcase, but she was too slow because Jonathan stepped into the room and grabbed it from her. "I've got it."

"Uh, thank you." She followed him outside and down the steps to her Lexus. He stopped in front of the driver's side and Natalie clicked the open button on her remote, but Jonathan didn't move out of her path.

She hiked up her chin, and heat and confusion spiked anew through her when she met his wolf's gaze. She knew what she saw. Desire. He wanted her, but that wasn't new. She was certain he would be happy to have her back in his bed, but what then? Natalie wasn't prepared to give all of herself and get nothing back in return.

"Don't go," Jonathan whispered.

Natalie shook her head. "I appreciate you giving my company a recommendation to your mother. That was kind of you, but if you think I owe you some sort of payback…"

He frowned. "Of course not. I would never think

that, Natalie. I just want to talk to you." He paused several beats and added, "I miss you."

Those words were her undoing.

Jonathan hadn't meant to say that aloud, to let Natalie know how he truly felt, but now that the words were out there, he couldn't, wouldn't take them back. Because they were true. Seeing her sitting in his mother's sitting room made all those feelings come rushing to the surface. It hadn't helped that Natalie wore a deliciously short dress that showed off her legs while the V-neck of the print dress gave him an ample view of her cleavage. She looked amazing and the desire that always seemed to burn brightly between them was waiting to be unleashed again. However, he needed to take care not to hurt her. He was already on thin ice after his two previous fumbles.

"Can we talk?" he asked.

"Where?" She glanced back toward the main house.

He shook his head. "Not here. My house is up the road. Will you come with me?"

"Yes." She didn't hesitate. She was ready to share her feelings, too. It was time *she* pursued him.

He opened her car door, and she took her briefcase from him before sliding inside. "I'll be ahead of you in the Bentley." She glanced around and saw instead of driving his Ford F-450, he had the expensive super-car nearby.

Jonathan didn't realize he'd been holding his breath until a sigh of relief escaped his lips. He noticed his mother peering out the window at them, but didn't care.

He took several long strides to his Bentley and within seconds was climbing in and turning on the ignition. He pulled out of the driveway with Natalie following behind him.

His four-bedroom ranch-style home was several miles from his parents'. His parents had gifted him the land on his twenty-fifth birthday. At the time, Jonathan thought he wanted a family of his own. He even hired an architect to design his dream home, which he'd thought he and his ex-wife would share, but by the time the first shovel went into the ground, their marriage was over.

And this was the first time he was bringing a woman to his domain. Usually when he took a woman home, they went to her place, and after their mutual pleasure, he usually drove himself home *alone*. He never stayed over because he wanted to be in his own room at the end of each night. But with Natalie, they'd spent every night together and he hadn't wanted separate rooms. Most nights they'd stayed in his palatial suite. Having Natalie in his home was monumental, but somehow it didn't feel wrong.

He was frustrated as hell and maybe having her here would bring back his sanity. He pictured her warm and naked in his bed with plenty of time to explore and taste every inch of her. Oh yes, this was a good idea.

When he exited the Bentley, Natalie was already out of her car, looking up at the house with oversize double wood doors.

Natalie turned to him. "It's beautiful."

"Thank you," Jonathan said, and walked to the front

door. He didn't get to unlock it because his housekeeper was there opening the door.

"Thank you, Josie."

"Natalie, this is Josie, my housekeeper. She's been with our family for years."

"Pleasure to meet you," Natalie said.

"It's nice to meet you, too. I was just leaving to head up to the main house," Josie stated, grabbing her purse from the nearby console table. "Jonathan, I've left some steaks and asparagus for you to grill, potatoes are in the oven."

"Thank you," Jonathan said. Once Josie had gone, he turned to Natalie. Her awe was audible, and he watched her glance at the piano in the foyer and move inward to the formal living room with a floor-to-ceiling stone fireplace and morning area. Sunshine filtered through the kitchen windows and from the wall of glass doors, which showed a covered patio.

"Wow! You have a lovely home." A smile lit up her whole face and made him want to step closer to feel the warmth of it against his skin. "Who designed this place?"

Jonathan was bemused. "You don't think I had anything to do with it?" He removed his business jacket and tossed it over the leather sofa.

"Did you?"

He laughed. "Sort of. I hired an architect to design it, a general contractor to build it and, as for decorating, my mother helped me hire an interior designer."

"She did good," Natalie stated, and then her expression turned somber. "So, why did you want to talk to me?"

Jonathan took off his Stetson and placed it on the

console table. When he moved toward her, Natalie took several paces backward, *away* from him. He didn't want that. "What's wrong?"

"I'm here because we need to talk. *I* need to talk."

"All right." Jonathan stayed where he was. "I'm all ears."

She was silent for several beats. Jonathan sensed that whatever it was, it wasn't easy for her to say. "I've always had a crush on you, Jonathan."

"Natalie…"

She held up her hand. "Please let me finish. I need to say this."

He inclined his head for her to continue.

"It was a schoolgirl crush because you were my hero saving me from bullies, but I don't feel that way anymore."

Jonathan didn't know why, but hearing those words made his stomach plunge and he felt like he might be sick.

"What I meant to say is that my crush developed into feelings that a woman has for a man," Natalie continued. "Feelings that were enhanced when we became lovers in Galveston. I want to see where we can go beyond the bedroom."

Jonathan was stunned. This talk wasn't going how he envisioned. He was usually in control of most situations, but with Natalie he never was. He, too, had feelings for her, but they were all jumbled, and he couldn't make sense of them. He also knew that if he let her walk out the door without at least trying, he would regret it. "I want to spend more time with you, Natalie."

"You do?"

"I do." He stalked to her and when he was within striking distance, he tangled his fingers in her braids and drew her close for a kiss.

It was impossible for Natalie to look away from Jonathan because his gaze imprisoned hers. Memories of the incredible week they spent together came flooding back. Oh God, she couldn't run away now and she wasn't sure she wanted to. He must have read her mind because his fingers tightened at her nape and prevented her escape. "Tell me you don't want this."

Natalie did want him, but he wasn't offering her commitment, either. He wanted to spend more time with her *in bed*. She desperately wished she was brave enough to tell him how she really felt—that she wanted marriage and babies and the white picket fence—but she wasn't. She didn't want to lose him, so she was willing to stay with him even though he wasn't offering her marriage or kids. When Jonathan bent his head and brushed his lips over hers, she let him. It was the softest of kisses and she hadn't expected it. She thought he was going to be all hunger and fire, but then another caress of his lips on hers came. And then another. She couldn't help her slight gasp and the parting of her lips, which allowed him to deepen the kiss. Slowly and thoroughly, he explored her mouth, and Natalie couldn't stop from kissing him back because it felt so good to be pressed against him. Soon they were lip to lip, breast to chest, hip to hip.

Of their own volition, her hips circled against him until they were grinding, and she could feel his hard arousal in his pants. They were teetering on the brink of him tumbling her to the sofa and taking her. She had to think. Natalie pulled back from him and to her relief he let her go.

"Is this why you brought me here?" Natalie asked. "For sex?"

"We're good together," Jonathan responded. "We should stop ignoring the obvious."

He was right. The man packed a serious sexual punch, but she wasn't going to make it easy for him, not after the last week of keeping her at arm's length. Everything couldn't be Jonathan's way, all the time.

"I ask you again, what do you want from me?"

Jonathan stared. "I want you in my bed, Natalie, for however long that is, but I'd like to keep this between us."

Natalie nodded. "I see. So you want to be bed buddies."

"Don't you?" When she began to speak, he interrupted her. "Before you say no, I want you to know I'm not trying to keep you a secret, but after the livestream everyone in town knew our business. I don't want that again. I'd like to keep this private. Can't we just see where this goes without putting a label on it? We tried to categorize it in Galveston and clearly that didn't work because we're both miserable. Let's put all our cards on the table. I like you. You like me."

"Are you sure about that?" she asked with a smirk.

He grinned. "I am."

She refused to be a foregone conclusion. "You think I'm easy."

"Absolutely not," he said, moving closer to her, "but I think you're hiding behind anger rather than admitting you want to be with me, too."

She hated that he was right.

His hands framed her face, and he was kissing her again. Plundering her mouth with his tongue. It seemed he couldn't get enough of kissing her, and the feeling was mutual. She *ached* to be with him, and when he pushed one thigh between her legs so he could press his hard length against her, *right there*, it felt so good, she began rocking uncontrollably against him to ease the need inside. Her nipples felt tight in her dress and begged for his mouth. She cried out when he took her jutting nipple into his mouth through the fabric and all.

"I want you," he muttered savagely, flicking the tight bud.

His hands dropped to the hem of her dress and hiked it high enough that he could push her panties aside. Then he slid a finger between her moist folds. She gripped his hand. Natalie wasn't sure whether it was to make him stop or make him go faster. Her hunger for this man was spiraling out of control. His thumb teased her sensitive nub while his fingers plunged in and out of her core.

Natalie released a sob of pleasure and Jonathan's mouth caught it. While his fingers worked her mercilessly, driving deeper inside her, Natalie arched to meet his hand.

"Oh, yes," she cried, trembling as an orgasm began to ravish her body.

"That's it," Jonathan rasped hoarsely. "Let go."

Natalie didn't have any other choice, especially when Jonathan's mouth crashed down on her in a hot, wet and carnal kiss that sent her over the edge. Her mouth broke free as cries of delight were torn from her. Jonathan held her body through the quakes until eventually she began to quiet. Only then did he straighten her panties and set her upright.

"I need a minute." Natalie rushed away from him and in the direction of what she hoped was the bathroom. She found it down the hall and immediately slammed the door, locking herself in. Gripping the sides of the sink, Natalie closed her eyes. She had climaxed on Jonathan's thigh in the middle of his living room like some randy teenager. What was wrong with her? She seemed to have no shame when it came to him. He could make her do anything, *feel* anything.

The schoolgirl crush she'd had morphed into feelings for a funny, sexy man she'd gotten to know in Galveston. She couldn't deny she wanted him, but she also wanted a future and Jonathan wasn't making her any promises that the fiery chemistry between them would lead to a commitment. She would be putting aside her dreams of a future to be with him, but the other option, to be without him, was something she couldn't fathom.

Several seconds later, she heard a soft knock on the door. "Natalie?"

She was afraid of getting her heart broken.

"Natalie, please open up."

"Go away."

He laughed. "I can't very well do that, it's my house."

She snorted. She would have to face him if she wanted to get out the door and back to the safety of her car. Slowly, Natalie stood upright and looked at herself in the mirror. Her eyes were glazed with passion. Passion that the man on the other side of the door seemed to bring out in her.

"Natalie," he called out to her again, and this time she opened the door.

He released a sigh of relief and to her surprise, held open his arms and Natalie rushed into them. He lowered his head, resting it against hers. "Please don't be embarrassed by what we shared. We enjoy each other. There's no shame in that." He lifted her chin so she was looking up at him. "Okay?"

She nodded. He assumed her turmoil was about their sexual encounter, but she was more worried about where they were going. Jonathan didn't want to put labels on them, and they only agreed to see each other and see where it went, which inevitably would lead to the bedroom, but could there be more? Or was she fooling herself into another sexual relationship with Jonathan? When would she finally get the courage to stand up and ask for what she wanted? Natalie didn't know. She only knew she was terrified of turning her back on the chance that she and Jonathan might become more than just lovers.

Twelve

"What do we do now?" Natalie asked Jonathan as she stared up at him with those beautiful deep brown eyes of hers. Her smile was unsure, but sexy even if she didn't know it. Jonathan would like nothing better than to take Natalie to his bedroom and make love to her all night long, but it was still early. His stomach was grumbling and reminded him he hadn't eaten since lunch.

"How about some dinner?" Jonathan inquired. "Josie left steaks for me to grill."

"You're going to cook for me?" She raised a skeptical eyebrow.

He laughed. "I'm no gourmet chef, but I can cook the basics including a mean steak."

"All right, then, yes. Dinner sounds good."

He smiled and headed for the spacious kitchen he

had designed. He went to the double-door Sub-Zero side-by-side refrigerator and found the two nicely marbled rib eyes Josie had seasoned. While he occupied himself heating up the grill, he noticed Natalie put her purse on the granite counter and slide her luscious bottom onto one of the high-backed bar stools at the large granite island.

"Would you like something to drink? I'm afraid I don't entertain much so I have some Perrier and beer."

"I'll have a beer."

He grinned. He was pleased she wasn't too pretentious to drink a beer with him. He went to the fridge and pulled out two Heinekens. After screwing off the top, he handed her an ice-cold one and kept the other for himself. He watched as she tipped the bottle back and took a generous swig. The way her lips cupped the rim had Jonathan thinking about how good Natalie was with her mouth.

He blinked and took a pull of beer and returned to his task of cooking their dinner. "So how do you feel about taking on the marketing for my mother's products?" Jonathan asked when his back was turned to Natalie. Although he hadn't asked his mother to give Natalie's firm the job, he strongly advocated for her to use the local company.

"I'm excited," Natalie replied. "It's going to be exactly the shot in the arm we need to help catapult us in the market. Having a Lattimore use our firm is huge, and I have you to thank for it."

He shook his head. "No, you don't. I might have recommended you, but my mother is a businesswoman.

She did her research and if she's decided she wants to use you, it's because it's the right thing for her brand."

Natalie grinned. "Thank you."

"For what?"

"You didn't have to put in a good word for me, not when you had no idea where we were going."

"I didn't do it as a quid pro quo and certainly not to get you back in my bed," Jonathan responded "You were passionate when you spoke about your company when we were in Galveston. I listened."

"I don't know what to make of you, Jonathan," Natalie replied. "One minute you're the distant and remote guy I slept with who can't be bothered to call or text me. And in the next breath, you're the man who's speaking on my behalf to his mother."

"I'm not that complicated," Jonathan responded as he checked on the potatoes baking in the convection oven. "I didn't text you because I was trying to honor our agreement. You have no idea, Natalie, how hard it was for me to stay away from you. When I saw you in Priceless, I realized that Galveston wasn't going to be enough. I wanted more, but I had already screwed up and you were angry with me."

Natalie drank more of her beer as she pondered her answer. "I was hurt and confused by your lack of communication."

Jonathan stopped making the dinner and moved toward Natalie at the counter. She didn't move away when he stepped between her legs and grasped her cheeks with his palms, forcing her to look at him. "I'm sorry." He didn't apologize often, but he needed to. Not communicating with Natalie made it easier to treat her as a casual hookup. He kept women at arm's length and he definitely didn't invite them into his home, his personal haven, but Natalie was different. He never wanted any woman as intensely as he did her—because he never wanted to feel the way he had after the failure of his marriage.

Desolate.

Broken.

Unworthy.

Realizing he wanted Natalie more than one week was a complication he hadn't foreseen; he didn't regret it, but he would have to be careful. Natalie wasn't someone who went from affair to affair.

She glanced up at him. "Thank you. I needed that."

He caressed her cheek. "Are we good now?"

She nodded.

"I'm going to finish up dinner." As hard as it was to slide from between her legs, Jonathan removed the asparagus from the fridge.

Soon, the steaks were sizzling on the grill. That's when Jonathan opened the glass doors so he could show Natalie the covered flagstone patio. His property faced the woods and led to a ravine in his own backyard.

The patio was his favorite place. It came with a wet bar, television and built-in stereo system facing a large infinity pool. Steps away was an outdoor stone-clad bar facing a wood-burning firepit with Adirondack chairs surrounding it. His favorite part of the fall season was sitting around the firepit with his brother or some of the ranch hands. He wondered if he would get the chance with Natalie.

They returned several minutes later so Jonathan could take the steaks off the grill and let them rest and put the asparagus in the broiler.

"The more I see the more impressed I am with your home."

"I designed it a long time ago." Jonathan's voice trailed off.

"When you were married?"

He nodded and began preparing their plates. "When I believed in happily-ever-after."

"And you don't believe in it now?"

"No." His answer was definite, and he noticed the smile fade on Natalie's face. But he had to be honest; he didn't want her to get any delusions that what was going on between them would lead to something more serious. He said he would try, but it wasn't a guarantee. "I will never marry again."

"I'm sorry to hear that. You could be missing out on something wonderful."

"That's because you have a fairy-tale version in your mind of what marriage is like," Jonathan responded. "But I know it's not all sunshine and roses."

He learned the hard way that marriage wasn't for him. It was committing to another person; he'd failed it. It was expressing his emotions that had been the hardest thing. It's not like his father or his grandfather showed any. They were men's men who didn't cry and got on with life. Jonathan was raised that way and he didn't know how to change. No matter how great Natalie was, he had no intention of making that mistake twice. He didn't do long-term commitment.

Jonathan's definitive response on marriage was certainly a buzzkill. Natalie finished off her beer and did her best not to show how disheartened she was to hear him say he would *never* marry again. If she continued down this path with him, it was quite possible she would be settling for the right now. The incredible sex and passion they shared was undeniable. The situation, however, was problematic because it went against her long-term goals and what she wanted for her future. She wanted a family of her own someday, but Jonathan was saying it wasn't on the table for him.

Yet she couldn't find the strength to walk out the door and away from him, a man she had wanted and lusted after since she was a teenager.

"Dinner's ready." Jonathan's words broke into her thoughts.

She smiled and slid off the bar stool, joining him at the table he'd set in the morning area between the living room and kitchen. He found some bottled water and poured them both glasses. Jonathan helped Natalie into her chair, and she couldn't help the awareness that rippled down her spine. Instead, she focused on the delicious meal in front of her. She cut into a bite of the steak and moaned at how buttery and succulent the meat was.

"This is amazing," she cooed.

Jonathan's chest puffed out. "I'm glad you like it.

Steak is one of the few things as a ranch hand you learn how to cook over an open fire."

"I'm afraid grilling isn't my thing," Natalie replied. "I leave that to my grandpa."

"Do you ever hear from your mother?" Jonathan asked, cutting into a piece of rib eye.

At his question, Natalie placed her fork and knife on the plate. Where had that come from?

She must have had a sour expression because Jonathan was apologizing seconds later. "I'm sorry. You don't have to answer that. I was curious."

Natalie took a deep breath and let the air out slowly. She knew he didn't mean any harm. It was a touchy subject she didn't often speak about.

"When I was younger, years went by, and we never heard from her. Eventually, when I was about twelve and going through puberty and finding where I fit in the world, my mother came back, said she was ready to be a mother again." Natalie picked up her fork and knife and resumed eating.

"And?"

"Six years had gone by." Natalie took a sip of water. "My grandparents had legally become my guardians and were in the process of officially adopting me. She put up a big stink and put me in a very awkward position of choosing between her and my grandparents. The only stable parents I'd ever known."

"I assume you chose your grandparents?" Jonathan asked.

Natalie nodded. "And my mother was angry. We didn't speak for many years and when I turned eighteen, she showed up again asking for forgiveness and hoping we could have some sort of relationship, but by then it was too late."

"What's your relationship with her now?"

"I get the odd birthday or Christmas card from her," Natalie responded, "but we're not close, if that's what you're asking."

Jonathan's hand clamped over hers and he squeezed it. "I'm sure it's been difficult for you."

"Yes, it has, but I've learned to accept who Phyllis is and that she will never be the mother I need her to be. But trust me, growing up that wasn't easy to accept."

"Thank you for sharing that with me."

Natalie lifted her head to meet his eyes and found her mouth dry because there was something else there. And it wasn't pity or compassion. Her heart raced. Sitting here with Jonathan in his home felt natural, like they were a couple. She had to scramble to remind herself that this attraction could burn out, but instead she got lost in his brown eyes.

Her body felt engulfed in flames. With effort, she smiled and reached for her glass of water. She was crazy to consider getting on this roller-coaster ride with him *again*.

"We should take these plates to the kitchen," Natalie said once she'd put her glass down.

She was about to rise when he said, "Leave it." His response was more of a command than a request and Natalie was about to sit down again, but Jonathan was already up and out of his chair, coming toward her.

When he reached her, his hand cupped her chin, and

he gently traced her lip with the tip of his finger. Once and then twice. On the second go-round, she couldn't resist flicking out her tongue and gliding it across his finger. She heard his swift indrawn breath.

Then he kissed her gently. She sank into the kiss, relishing every part of him she could touch with her lips and with her tongue. She ached to feel his skin against hers once more. He groaned and reached out quickly to lift her off her feet and before Natalie knew it, her legs were wrapped around his waist and he was carrying her down the hall.

Seconds later, he released her onto a sprawling king-size bed. "Are you okay with this?" Jonathan asked. "And what I can offer?"

Natalie knew she could walk away and that would be it, but she couldn't do it. Instead, she pulled him toward her and their mouths collided. She moaned when Jonathan's hands explored her body and he uncinched the belt holding her dress together. He lifted her up long enough to push the fabric aside and unclasp her bra, releasing her full breasts, which were achy for him.

He was everything she wanted. She cried out when he sucked one of her painfully tight nipples into his warm mouth. A low flame ignited in her belly, especially when he slipped off her shoes and ran his hands up her legs to her panties. He slid them down and off until she was naked, hot and ready for him.

"I've missed seeing you," he murmured.

"I want to see you, too." She reached for his button-down shirt to start unbuttoning, but he pushed her hands away.

"Later," he said, sliding down her body. "It's been too long. I need to taste you."

Natalie felt his warm hands on her thighs as he kissed his way lower. She splayed her legs wide to make room for him and before she knew it, he was licking her core and holding her to his mouth in the most carnal position imaginable. Sobs of pleasure escaped her lips as his tongue caressed her with swirls and licks until she started to tremble.

"Jonathan, *please*… I need you."

He broke free to come up and brace above her, she felt his hard length in his pants and immediately began attacking the buttons on his shirt. Once they were undone, he shrugged it off and allowed Natalie to slide her hands over the damp heat of his broad chest. Then she was unbuckling the belt, unzipping his pants and roughly pulling them over his slender hips.

She wanted him *now*.

He left for a moment to reach for the box of condoms in his nightstand. When he returned, he was already sheathed. He grabbed her hips firmly to him and she gasped. The look of raw lust in his eyes made her spellbound. She thought she was going to die if he didn't make love to her. And then he thrusted. *Hard*.

"Jonathan." Her body instantly locked on his and she clutched him closer, her legs parting so he could fill her completely.

"Hell, Natalie!" he ground out, and frantically began moving inside her.

"Yes," she cried, twisting beneath him. He felt so good. And when he drove deeper still and pumped faster, she rose to meet every fierce thrust. Her hands were greedy for him, grasping his taut bottom. "Oh yes!"

She didn't want him to stop. She wished they could go on and on, pounding together as one. She felt completely free, but soon her orgasm came crashing toward her. When she reached the peak, ecstasy coursed through her, and she shattered.

Jonathan growled and kept thrusting harder and deeper. His eyes were wild as he stared at her. And his skin glistened from the effort as he strained to fight the rising tide, but it was too much. A guttural shout escaped his lips, and he broke. Natalie rode the wave with him as aftershocks rocked his body.

It felt good to be here in Jonathan's home where she belonged.

Thirteen

"Look who is finally free to spend time with the boys," Jonathan's brother, Jayden, said when he met him and some of the ranch hands for drinks on Friday evening. It had been a long day. Several bulls had gotten loose and crossed over into Grandin land and it had taken a lot of wrangling to corral them back to the Lattimore ranch. Jonathan told his crew he would treat them all to some beers for their hard work at the local bar in town. His men had been appreciative, and Jayden decided to join.

"What's that supposed to mean?" Jonathan asked, taking a pull of his beer.

"This week, whenever anyone suggested going out after work, you always had plans," Jayden replied.

"And?"

"You're a bachelor, same as me," Jayden said. "Or maybe you're not." He lowered his voice and pulled Jonathan away from the group so they could talk privately. "Have you been getting busy with Natalie Hastings again?"

Jonathan glanced around him to make sure no one heard him. "You need to keep your voice down. I don't want anyone to hear your speculations."

"They aren't speculation if they're true," Jayden returned, "and your refusal to answer is revealing."

"Fine." Jonathan sighed. "I'll admit Natalie and I have rekindled what we had in Galveston."

"Meaning what? You're hooking up?"

"Something like that."

Jayden snorted. "Do you have any idea what you're doing, Jonathan? Natalie is not the kind of girl you mess around with."

"I know that," Jonathan stated. He thought about it all the time. He never wanted to hurt her. "I have been up-front with Natalie about my feelings on commitment and marriage, for that matter. She's under no illusions."

"Are you sure about that?" Jayden inquired. "Because sometimes women think they can change you."

"Natalie is not like that."

"So, you trust her?"

Jonathan paused before answering because he'd never really thought about it until now, but he did. Natalie was honest and truthful, unlike Anne, who was manipulative and deceitful. "Yes, I do."

Jayden shrugged. "Well, that's saying something

because you haven't trusted a woman in a long time. Maybe you should consider whether hooking up is all you want from Natalie."

"Don't go reading more into this than what I've said. Matrimony is not for me." Jonathan was adamant that marriage, a family, the whole bit was no longer in the cards for him. Those dreams died when he stroked the pen on his divorce papers.

"If you say so, but methinks you doth protest too much," Jayden replied.

On his drive home back to the ranch, Jonathan wondered if Jayden was right. Was he leading Natalie on? It certainly wasn't his intention. He'd been as plain as he could be about what he was willing to offer, and he wouldn't promise her a ring. But maybe he should end things and allow Natalie to find a nice guy who'd give her a house with a white picket fence and two point five children?

The thought rang hollow. He ran his hand over his head. He was in quite the dilemma. Let Natalie go so she could find someone worthy of her or allow the flame between them to burn out of its own accord. When his phone rang and he glanced down and saw Natalie's name, he knew it was the latter.

Natalie couldn't believe she was seeing Jonathan. Since the day she went to the Lattimore ranch to meet his mother, they had been together nearly every day. That's when she and Brent weren't working on their plans for how to help Barbara Lattimore market her new line of culinary products.

No one knew about their relationship. Jonathan had made his feelings known that he had no intention of getting married again. *Ever.* They'd fallen into a routine of hanging out either at her cottage in town or as they'd done this past weekend, she stayed at his ranch from Friday night until early Monday morning. They cooked or watched television, or she listened to Jonathan play the piano. Eventually, Natalie would return home for a change of clothes and to get herself ready for the workweek.

She was addicted to the sexy rancher, and although they were acting like a couple, she knew Jonathan didn't want anything more from her. As for the explosive passion they shared, it hadn't diminished. In her opinion, it had become stronger the more time they spent together. Why couldn't he see what a great life they could have if he only gave marriage a chance?

It didn't help that she was on her way to meet up with Chelsea at Natalie Valentine's bridal shop on Saturday. Chelsea's wedding was in several months and her best friend was looking for the most amazing dress. Chelsea wanted to get a general idea of the dress she wanted before bringing her mother and sisters.

"I want to listen to my own voice and select what I like for my big day," Chelsea had said, and now Natalie was at the shop to be Chelsea's wingwoman.

When she arrived, her best friend was already there talking with one of the shopgirls. She glanced around the brightly lit room with racks of white, ivory and blush wedding dresses of all shapes and styles. Stylish high-backed chairs and tufted benches were in abundance around the store. It had been Natalie's dream to be a bride one day; she just wouldn't be married to her groom of choice.

"Chelsea!" Natalie put on her best smile because she was indeed happy for her friend.

"Natalie! I'm so glad you're here," Chelsea said, rushing toward her and enveloping her in a hug. She looked gorgeous in a simple shift dress, but classic Chelsea because she was wearing cowboy boots.

"So am I. I can't wait to get this party started," Natalie gushed.

"Natalie, this is Miriam. She's going to be my stylist today," Chelsea said of the sleek blonde in a simple black shift dress.

"Pleasure to meet you," Natalie replied.

"Same," Miriam replied, and handed Natalie a glass of champagne as well.

"I was already telling Miriam that I'm getting married in December and it'll be cool out," Chelsea started, "I'm thinking a long-sleeved dress might be in order."

"I love a long sleeve," Natalie replied. "It's classic."

"Have you decided what type of silhouette you would like?" Miriam inquired. "Fit and flare, mermaid, ball gown or sheath?"

"As slim as I am, I'd get lost in a ball gown," Chelsea responded with a laugh.

"I couldn't agree more," Miriam responded. "I honestly think a sheath would be amazing. And if you like, there are dresses with a detachable overskirt. You can have the skirt on for the ceremony to give you the sense of occasion and the sheath as your reception dress so you can move around, have fun and dance."

"I'm definitely open to seeing them," Chelsea said, and went over to a mannequin with a gorgeous sheath dress made with handmade lace. "I definitely want to try on this one."

"Certainly. Come with me and I'll get you set up in a fitting room and then we'll get you in the first dress."

While Chelsea slipped into the confection, Natalie perused the store. She couldn't help imagining the dress she might choose someday if she were walking down the aisle. God, she wished it was to Jonathan. Natalie knew a ball gown wouldn't suit her curvy figure. She would definitely need straps to keep up her full bosom, but figured a fit and flare or mermaid gown would work best. Then Chelsea came out of the dressing room and Natalie was speechless.

Her best friend looked like a princess in a long-sleeved lace sheath dress with an illusion V-neck and corset bodice.

"You look stunning, Chelsea."

"Do I?" Chelsea asked, her pale cheeks turning rosy at the compliment.

"Absolutely."

"Come." Miriam led Chelsea to a dais and her friend stepped on and stared at her reflection in the three-way mirror. Chelsea spun around and looked at the dress from all angles.

"Wow!" Chelsea's chocolate-brown eyes grew large. "Do you see how great this dress makes my butt look?"

Natalie laughed. Chelsea always spoke her mind.

It's why they were besties. "You would blow Nolan's mind in that dress."

"I would, wouldn't I? But I can't pick the first dress I've ever tried on," Chelsea admonished. She looked down at the stylist. "Let's try on a few more."

An hour later, Chelsea had changed back into her sheath dress and cowboy boots. Of all the dresses she tried on, her heart was set on the first. She planned on bringing her mom and sisters in to see it. "How about a cocktail? After all that girlie stuff, I could use a real drink."

"Sounds fabulous." Natalie was dying to talk to her about what transpired between her and Jonathan the last few days anyway.

They ended up in the bar area sitting at high tops at Sheen. The new restaurant made entirely of glass had become a favorite among the locals since it opened.

Natalie ordered a martini, while Chelsea opted for a whiskey. She was a cowgirl through and through.

"So." Chelsea leaned back in the chair to look at Natalie. "I loved my hour of being the center of attention, but you know girlie things aren't my thing. What I'm dying to know is, how has it been going between you and Jonathan?"

"Cutting to the chase, huh?" Natalie asked, raising a brow.

"You know it." Chelsea leaned forward on her forearms with a wide grin. "Now stop stalling and dish. Did you or didn't you put the moves on the oldest Lattimore son?"

Natalie laughed. "I didn't need to. He did."

"Really?" Chelsea tipped back her whiskey. "Do tell."

"He recommended me to Barbara to help with the marketing of the new products for her culinary line. She asked me to the ranch and when I was there, who should show up?"

"Jonathan," Chelsea finished.

Natalie nodded. "After our meeting, he asked me to talk. And let's just say talking led to more and then some."

Chelsea rubbed her hands together. "Sounds sinful."

"But…there's more."

"Go on."

"He told me he doesn't want to get married again."

"Urgh!" Chelsea threw her head back in annoyance. "People say that all the time, but that doesn't mean you can't try to change his mind. Hell, you're already halfway there."

"How do you figure that?"

"You got him off his game," Chelsea replied. "Didn't you tell me he usually has casual relationships with women?"

Natalie nodded.

"You're more than that, Nat. He spent the entire week with you in Galveston. And guess what? He couldn't stop thinking about you. And now that you're both back in Royal, he's become fixated with you. I'm telling you—you got that man by the…"

"Don't say it," Natalie said, wagging her finger at Chelsea's bold tongue.

Chelsea shrugged. "I'm merely stating the facts.

Jonathan says he only wants to hook up, but is that all you two do when you're together?"

"No," Natalie said. "We talk, we laugh, we cook, watch television."

"Sounds like dating to me. Jonathan just doesn't know it yet."

"I suppose, but he hasn't taken me out on the town, either."

"How do you feel about that?"

Natalie shrugged. "He told me he didn't want the tongues wagging about us like they did after the livestream."

Natalie peered at Chelsea. "But you could be right." Her best friend might be onto something. Jonathan talked a good game and said he wasn't interested in a serious or committed relationship, but his *actions* showed her that they were having one. The million-dollar question was, where would it lead?

Fourteen

"Thank you for inviting me out for a ride," Natalie said on Saturday as she sat astride a beautiful palomino horse. The Lattimores owned a plethora of beautiful prize-winning horses. She was fortunate to be able to ride one of them.

"You're welcome," Jonathan replied. He looked sexy and dangerous in his rugged jeans, plaid shirt, Stetson and cowboy boots.

Jonathan often talked about his love of the open range, but this was the first time he was allowing Natalie to explore his world. Last night she'd been surprised when he hadn't come over to her cottage. Sure, she and Brent had a long night wining and dining a client, but usually Natalie and Jonathan spent their evenings together in bed.

Natalie had tried not to feel abandoned or unwanted. He had no clue that she had issues of abandonment because her mother left her. Even though her grandparents adopted Natalie and Phyllis eventually returned, the stain was still there and Natalie had never been able to blot it out no matter how hard she tried.

And so, when she'd come home to an empty house, she resigned herself to the notion of sleeping in her bed alone, but then Jonathan called, and they stayed up talking on the phone for hours like she had when she was a teenager. That's when he'd asked her to meet him this afternoon at the ranch.

"It really is majestic," Natalie said when, after an hour, they stopped so the horses could rest, get water and a treat. She needed it, too. She was no horsewoman and only rode upon occasion. She would definitely be sore tomorrow.

"I'm glad you think so," Jonathan said. "This is one of my favorite spots. It's why we've stopped. I brought a picnic for us." He untied a picnic basket from his horse Beauty's back and brought it along with a pillow and blanket to a patch of grass.

"You did?" Natalie tried to keep her tone calm, even though joy surged through her at Jonathan's romanticism. It was definitely a date, though she doubted he thought of it that way. And who cares if it wasn't in town; Natalie would soak up spending time with Jonathan while she could.

She watched as he laid out the blanket on the grass underneath a large oak tree and opened the basket. Inside was a delicious charcuterie board of meats from salami to prosciutto, soft and hard cheeses, fig jam, pepper jelly, nuts and fruit.

"Come, sit down and eat," Jonathan said when she stared down at him in bemusement because there was no way he'd made the picnic himself. He had to have help. Surely that meant he cared to go through all the trouble?

She slid to her knees and joined him on the blanket. "I'm impressed with your efforts, Mr. Lattimore."

He turned to her laugh. "You don't think these hardworking hands—" he lifted his large hands roughened from fieldwork in the air "—put this meal together?"

"Absolutely not." Natalie laughed. "But I'm enjoying it all the same." She put some brie and fig jam on a cracker and plopped it in her mouth.

"How about some champagne to wash that down?" Jonathan asked, reaching for the bottle of Veuve and popping the cork.

"I think I can go for that."

He poured them each two plastic champagne flutes and handed her one. "Cheers."

She tapped her flute with his and easily finished the glass in one swig.

"More?" Jonathan inquired.

"Are you trying to get me drunk so you can have your way with me?"

He grinned and his eyes were alight with mischief. "Yeah, is it working?"

"I'll need a few more of these," she said, holding up her flute.

He filled up her glass and they continued their charcuterie feast until the board was damn near empty, along with the bottle of champagne. "Ah, that was amazing." Natalie sighed in contentment and laid her head back on the pillow.

"I concur." Jonathan slid beside her on the pillow. He curled his arm around her waist and hugged her closer against him. She felt so content being held by him. She would take whatever stolen moments she could get, because she didn't want to pressure him into a commitment. On the other hand, she was afraid that moments like this might make her stay with him whether he chose to never marry or have kids. It was all too much; she closed her eyes and drifted off to sleep in the safety and comfort of his arms.

Natalie stretched as she woke from her nap and when she did, she realized someone was against her back. Jonathan.

And he was *hard*.

"Oh," she gasped, and began to move away, but his arm was around clutching her back to his front. Natalie felt the unmistakable shape of him against her bottom.

Natalie tried to wiggle away, but a grumble of dissatisfaction rumbled in his chest. "You're only making it worse."

"Well, what do you suggest we do about it?" Natalie asked. They were in the wide open where anyone could see them if they passed by.

As if reading her thoughts, Jonathan whispered, "No one comes out here, Natalie. Not my family at least. It's kind of like, my spot, you know. And as for my men, they're working hundreds of miles away."

She turned sideways and faced him. "What are you saying exactly?"

He grinned like the Cheshire cat. "That if you wanted to help relieve me of this condition…we're *alone*."

Natalie sat upright. She'd never had sex in public where anyone might see them. It was dangerous. Risky. But when she was with Jonathan, he made her unafraid to live out her wildest fantasies, and making love to her man out in the open would definitely qualify. Jonathan was the man she'd crushed on and had now fallen for; there wasn't anything she wouldn't do for him.

Jonathan watched the indecision on Natalie's round face. He sensed she wanted to live dangerously but was afraid. He would never want her to do anything she wasn't completely comfortable with, so it surprised him when she began unbuttoning her shirt. He was transfixed watching her as she unhurriedly undid each button. When she was free, she pulled the shirt free from the jeans he'd been dying to get her out of since she first arrived at his house. The damn things looked as if they'd been sprayed on and showed off her fabulous *ass*ets.

He sat still only as long as she unclipped her bra and shrugged out of it, sliding the straps off her arms until she threw it on the blanket. Then he rose on his haunches to whip off his shirt and stood to remove his jeans. He helped Natalie to her feet and when she looked down, he cupped her chin.

"You don't have to do this, Nat." He used a nickname he'd only recently started using.

Her eyelashes fluttered open, and she pierced him with her gaze. "I want to." She unzipped her jeans and with one fell swoop took them and her panties off until she was standing naked in front of him.

Jonathan nearly fell backward at being faced with her beauty in the daylight with the sun and flowers all around her; she looked like a goddess. He took her hand in his and laid her back down against the pillow and blanket and looked his fill. He wondered when he would ever tire of her delectable body.

"I can't wait to put my mouth on you," he said, using his fingertips to brush across her abdomen.

"Good, because I can't wait to claim every inch of you." She slid her hand up the back of his neck and, exerting pressure, pulled his head down to hers. Their kiss was wild, raw and incendiary. It spoke of greed and a need between them that had yet to be quenched.

Jonathan's lips left hers long enough for him to take an erotic bite at her nape. Natalie shivered underneath him, but she was claiming him like she wanted, too. She slid her mouth across one of his nipples and then treated the other to the same attention. He gathered her braids behind her neck and exposed her throat so he could take gentle nips of the soft flesh. She arched her body in surrender, mashing her mound against the firm ridge of his erection.

Jesus, if she kept that up, he'd be taking her swiftly, and he wanted to savor her because the longer this went on the wilder she was becoming. Jonathan didn't know how long he would be able to keep this up without wanting to make her *his* permanently. And that was not to be borne.

And so he did the only thing he could: he feasted on her.

Jonathan made her crazy. The way he'd taken her outdoors on the blanket had been nothing short of epic. Natalie was still thinking about it on Monday in her office.

She'd welcomed every moment of his thick intrusion as he stretched her. The way they fit, the delicious friction of his skin on hers. The suck of his lips on her neck, his fingers at her core. Even now, sitting in her office, Natalie still felt the way he ground himself into her, hip to hip, until a wave of orgasm threatened to take her under. There was no way she could have been as open and fearless making love outdoors if she hadn't been with Jonathan, the man she loved.

"Earth to Natalie!"

Natalie blinked out of her erotic daydream to find Brent standing in her doorway.

"Must have been some hot weekend," Brent stated.

Natalie fanned herself. "You have no idea." She reached for the water bottle on her desk and drank generously.

"I was hoping we could go over the best companies we should present to Barbara Lattimore for her brand."

"Yes, of course, come on in," Natalie said. "I was thinking how we could team up with some of the big-box retailers to get her products in their stores."

"I think positioning her as the next Pioneer Woman

or something of that sort is the way to go. There's always room for one more at the top."

"I agree with you. Barbara has the down-home Southern feel that will resonate with the public. However, I was looking at her website and I feel like it needs an overhaul to make it fresh and more inviting and user-friendly for the home cook to find recipes. But even more, we need her to have an online shop where readers can buy her products, including those signed by Barbara herself."

"All fantastic ideas, Natalie. I don't know if your tryst with Jonathan had anything to do with us getting this contract, but I'm so thankful."

"I'm glad I could help," Natalie replied, and watched her partner leave her office.

She'd recently confided in Brent about her and Jonathan's vacation fling. She felt it was only the right thing to do, especially since they'd begun seeing each other since returning to Royal. She suspected Brent might worry about the effect this could have on their business, but Natalie wasn't.

The contract with Barbara Lattimore would be ironclad; their lawyers were putting the finishing touches on the document now. Business was business. She had only met Jonathan's mother once, but she struck her as someone of the highest integrity and no way would she fire H & W Marketing because Natalie and Jonathan ended their affair.

Was she nervous about when that day came? Absolutely. But until that day came, she would take this precious time with Jonathan and enjoy it while she could.

She loved him and if he gave them a chance, they could have the fairy-tale ending deep down in her gut she knew they were destined for.

Fifteen

"Thank you all for coming," Alexa said when all of the Grandins—Victor Jr., his wife, Bethany, and their four children, Vic, Chelsea, Layla and Morgan—filtered into the Lattimore family room on Friday evening.

His sister had summoned both families to a meeting to give them an update on where they stood with Heath Thurston's claim.

"Have you discovered more information about my dad?" Victor Jr. inquired.

"I'll let Jonas speak on this matter," Alexa replied and turned to Jonas Shaw, the PI they hired to unearth the truth.

Jonas was an older gentleman with salt-and-pepper hair and had a perpetual five-o'clock shadow. He was tall and slim and was more comfortable in jeans than a suit.

"As you know, I had a lead on your grandfather Augustus's former secretary, a Sylvia Stewart. Unfortunately, she's a travel junkie and is off on some wilderness trek. I was finally able to make contact with her briefly, but she was in a remote area with bad cell service. She's agreed to talk to me when she returns."

"That's promising," Layla commented. As the middle daughter in the Grandin family, with long blond hair and blue eyes, she had always been the stunner. Jonathan knew both their families hoped he would have married any of the Grandins, but he'd fallen hook, line and sinker for Anne's schemes.

"As you all know, I have confirmed, after extensive research, that the deed promising Heath and Thurston's mother, Cynthia, the oil rights is legitimate," Alexa stated.

"I still don't believe it," her father responded.

"I'm afraid so, Daddy," Alexa stated. "We can no longer put our heads in the sand and act like this isn't happening."

Jonas stood and spoke. "I've also confirmed Augustus and Victor Sr. had both properties surveyed for oil a year before the rights were signed over to Cynthia."

"What has Augustus said about all of this, Alexa?" Victor Jr. inquired.

"Not much," Alexa answered. "When I asked him about the survey, he denied knowing anything about it."

"He may not be lying," Ben Lattimore stated. "His memory is failing." Jonathan looked at his dad. His dad and grandfather had always shared a close bond, and Ben refused to think ill of Augustus.

"Are you sure about that, Ben?" Victor Jr. asked.

"Of course I am. You've seen him."

"Here's where we are," Jonas said, getting everyone back on track. "The surveys were inconclusive."

"See, there's no oil underneath our lands," Vic, the only son in the Grandin clan, stated. "So there's nothing to deal with."

"I'm with Vic on this one," Jayden replied.

Jonathan wasn't surprised. Jayden and Vic had been inseparable growing up. If you saw one, the other wasn't far behind.

"Inconclusive doesn't mean no oil," Jonathan's father said, sadly. "We need to talk to Sylvia and see if she can shed any light on this mess."

"I agree with Mr. Lattimore. We need more info from Sylvia and I'm working on that as fast as I can," Jonas stated.

There was a lot of conversation back and forth between the families. Eventually, they decided to have Jonas look into finding if there were any other surveys. He promised to get back with them on next steps. Jonathan was happy when the Grandin family filed out and it was just the Lattimore clan.

"Maybe I should talk to Dad again," his father said, looking around the room. "See if he can remember anything."

"Why upset Grandfather any further?" Jonathan asked, folding his arms across his chest. "It's like you said, his memory is deteriorating. He's ninety-six years old, for Christ's sake."

His father sighed and plopped down on the sofa. "I just hate that we're all in this mess because of something out of any of our control."

Alexa walked over and crouched down in front of him. "We'll figure it out, Daddy. No matter the outcome. I'll help the families navigate it."

He caressed her cheek. "Thanks, baby girl."

Jonathan glanced down at his watch and frowned. He wanted to go over to Natalie's, but it was much later than he'd imagined; the family meeting had taken longer than expected. He had an early morning tomorrow, so he would see her another day.

"Problem?" his mother asked, coming to his side.

Jonathan shook his head. "Not at all. It's later than I thought."

"Did you have plans?"

Her question sounded innocent, but it seemed like she was fishing. Jonathan knew she suspected something was going on between him and Natalie, but she hadn't pressed. "No. Early morning is all. I'll see everyone later." He waved good-night to the family and after kissing his mother on the cheek made a quick exit before she could start the Spanish Inquisition.

Once outside, he exhaled; he'd escaped the firing squad. Reaching in his back pocket, he pulled out his cell and dialed Natalie's number. She answered several seconds later with a breathy "Hello."

"Hey, babe."

"Are you on your way?"

"Afraid not. It's late and I have to get up early for a ranch meeting."

"Oh, all right." He heard the disappointment in her voice, and he felt the same. He liked falling asleep with Natalie in his arms and even more waking up and making love to her in the wee hours of the morning.

"I promise I'll make it up to you."

"I'm holding you to it."

He ended the call and walked to his truck with a smile. He and Natalie had only been seeing each other for a couple of weeks but she'd quickly become important to him. For nearly a decade, he'd kept his relationships casual because there had never been a woman he wanted to try to make a go of it with, but Natalie was chipping away at his resistance to commitment. Jonathan said he'd never marry again, but if anyone made him want to be wrong, it was Natalie.

"I'm so happy you could come out with me, sweetheart," Natalie's grandmother said when they met to go to the farmers' market on Saturday morning.

Every week, farmers and vendors from Royal and the surrounding counties came to sell fresh produce, delightful treats, handmade items, plants, jewelry and sometimes even artwork underneath the shaded tree canopy of the town square.

"Sorry I've been MIA the last couple of weeks, Mimi," Natalie replied.

"It's fine. You're an adult now. I know you have your own life," her grandmother said.

"But I always have time for you," Natalie said, circling her arm into her grandmother's. "What do you want to pick up today?"

"Oh, a little bit of this and a little bit of that." Her grandmother loved stopping at different vendors and seeing which vegetables or fruits looked good before deciding what to buy.

Natalie was much more decisive, going with a list of exactly what she wanted.

They stopped at a vendor selling fresh peaches and plums. Natalie was testing the fruit out for firmness when she heard someone calling her name. She was surprised to turn around and see Barbara Lattimore with Jonathan not far from her side.

"Natalie." Barbara came toward her and kissed both of her cheeks. "What a surprise running into you here. Isn't it, Jonathan?" She looked up at her son.

Natalie was thinking the same thing. Jonathan told her he was working this morning, which is why he hadn't come over to her cottage last night. Instead, he was shopping with his mother. Did he not want to spend time with her? If not, he only had to say so. They had been spending an awful lot of time together. She understood if he wanted some breathing room.

Natalie plastered on her best smile. "Barbara, have you met my mother, Claudette Hastings?"

"Oh yes, we know each other," her grandmother replied, patting Natalie's arm. "Barbara and I sit on the same auxiliary committee for the church."

"I had no idea," Natalie replied.

"That's because you need to come to church more often," her grandmother chastised. "Then you could meet that fine young man I told you about," her grand-mother said, giving Jonathan the once-over. She had told her mimi she was moving on from her crush, but that was far from the case.

"I declare." Barbara touched her chest and her eyes narrowed in on Natalie. "I had no idea you were dating someone."

Natalie could only imagine what was running through Jonathan's mother's head, that Natalie was doing double duty and dipping out on her son, which wasn't true. "Oh, I'm not dating anyone at the moment, Barbara," Natalie said, and prayed her nose didn't extend like Pinocchio's. "I've just been focusing on my business."

"Is that right?" Barbara hazarded a sideways glance at her son, who remained quiet and stalwart at her side. Natalie wondered what he was thinking. Was he jealous that her grandmother was trying to fix her up? When Jonathan didn't speak, she said, "These fruits look amazing, Claudette. Did you see the other peaches Mrs. Mabelle has two tents away?"

"No, I hadn't," her grandmother stated.

"Allow me to show you." Barbara led her grand-mother away, but not before giving Natalie and Jon-athan a conspiratorial wink. Did she know they had been seeing each other since she'd revealed her match-making scheme?

"What are you doing here?" Natalie whispered underneath her breath as several townspeople were mill-ing around the square. She wanted to appear casual at their chance meeting and not portray any emotion or feeling at being this close to Jonathan. "I thought you had to work?"

Jonathan smiled as he glanced around him and murmured, "I did, but my mother asked me to come with her when I was done because she needed my brawn because she was buying cases of fruit for the annual Bake-Off coming up next week."

Natalie nodded as several people she knew passed by them.

"Am I going to see you later?"

"That depends," Jonathan whispered. "Do you have a date tonight with someone I should know about?"

Natalie chuckled. "Are you jealous?"

"Why would I be?" Jonathan said. "You're mine. I own your orgasms."

Natalie blushed at his incendiary words. For someone who wasn't interested in a relationship, he certainly sounded possessive. "Jonathan!"

"I missed you last night."

Underneath her lashes, Natalie glanced up at him. "You did?"

"You know I did. Let me finish up with my mother and stuff at the ranch, then I'll come by tonight. I'm all yours until Monday morning."

"I like the sound of it."

"Good. And you better steer clear of your grandmother's matchmaking. Otherwise, I might have to spank you later."

"Promises. Promises," Natalie whispered, and Jonathan laughed as he sauntered away. She was beginning to suspect Jonathan might be equally invested in their relationship despite his denials to the contrary.

It was hot as blazes in Natalie's garage by the time she dropped off her grandmother and got to her favorite Saturday afternoon activity. But she wasn't going to let it deter her from taking the old maple slant-front desk she had eventually gone back to purchase at Priceless and turning it into a wedding present for Chelsea. It was going to take some elbow grease, which is why she'd put on cutoff jean shorts and a tank top.

A lot had to be done. She removed the old hardware and then cleaned the desk with some mineral spirts using a microfiber cloth so she could fix any blemishes.

Going with the grain, she used sandpaper to take off the topcoat with her sander. Then she used a sanding sponge and hand-sanded the corners and edges. When she was done, she went over it one more time with her sander and another cleaning with mineral spirits. The desk was already looking better.

She was in the middle of priming the desk when she heard the roar of a truck engine come up her driveway. Natalie stood upright and saw Jonathan come swaggering toward her.

She grinned. "What are you doing here so early?"

"I finished my work, but you didn't answer your phone, so I thought I'd come by and see what you were up to." Jonathan pulled her toward him and into a long searing kiss. When he released her, he glanced around the garage. "What are you working on?"

"Remember that piece I was admiring at Priceless? Well, I'm refinishing it."

"Need any help?"

"Sure. You can help me prime it," Natalie said. "But we need to tape it off first."

"All right."

Natalie watched with glee as Jonathan unbuttoned the plaid shirt he'd been wearing and placed it over a chair, leaving him in one of his muscle T-shirts. She loved when he wore them because they showed off his broad chest and chiseled abs. Working on the ranch ensured there wasn't an inch of flab on Jonathan's abdomen. Natalie handed him some blue tape.

"So how did the meeting go with you and the Grandins last night?" Natalie inquired as they worked in tandem to place tape around the edges of the desk.

"Not much has changed," Jonathan replied as he filled her in on what happened.

"That sounds positive," Natalie said. She passed him one of the bottles of primer along with a face mask. "We're going to use this to spray the desk and then we'll sand it again."

"Sounds like a lot of steps," Jonathan said, putting the mask on, but he did as she instructed.

They sprayed the desk, and it was time to sand again. She wiped the sweat from her forehead with a rag tucked in her back pocket. Jonathan's T-shirt was soaked as well, but he'd never looked hotter. If she had her druthers, she'd strip him naked, and they'd make love on the floor of her garage. That's how oversexed Natalie felt when Jonathan was around.

She used a sanding sponge to clean the desk one more time before applying another coat of primer.

"Okay, I think this thing is ready for paint. We need to put a cloth down to protect the garage floor." She walked over and grabbed a few paint-splattered cloths sitting in a nearby bin.

"I have to tell you, Nat, this is an awful lot of work to go through. You call this fun?" Jonathan said as he lifted the desk so Natalie could place a drop cloth underneath it.

Natalie lifted her head up and smiled at him. "The reward at the end is so worth it because you have a beautiful new piece." She wished Jonathan could see that their relationship could be made new again exactly like the desk. With time and a little care, love could be their reward. She walked over to grab the gallon of blue paint she was using to paint the desk along with two paintbrushes. "One for you—" she gave Jonathan a brush "—and one for me.

"You'll see." Natalie squatted to the floor and commenced to lightly stroke the paint onto the legs of the desk. Jonathan imitated her actions on the opposite side. Along the way, Natalie used her sanding sponge to go over each coat of paint. In the end, when the legs and front of the desk were complete, Natalie cleaned the top and then stained it with an oil-based wood finish and finished it with a polyurethane seal coat. Jonathan was a godsend and helped her install the new gold hardware pulls.

Hours later, Natalie stood back to admire the finished product. "So." She gave a sideways glance to Jonathan. "What do you think?"

Jonathan nodded. "I have to tell you, Nat. When I got here, I thought you were out of your mind to take on a project like this but seeing the result, I'm impressed with your work."

Natalie beamed with pride. "You are?"

"Oh, absolutely," Jonathan said. "Your attention to detail is top-notch. I think Chelsea is going to be really happy with the desk and those other two pieces from Galveston."

"I hope so," Natalie said. She wanted to give her best friend something from the heart because Chelsea had always been there for Natalie and never abandoned her. "How about a beer? I think you deserve one."

"A beer and then a shower," Jonathan said.

"In that order?" Natalie asked.

He laughed. "Oh yeah. Because after the shower, I think we're going to need a nap."

Natalie smiled, knowing that the last thing they were about to do was sleep.

Natalie was feeling good. Better than she'd ever felt. Life was going splendid. H & W Marketing was going better than ever. The signed contracts had been couriered back to Barbara Lattimore's attorney and to her surprise, Jonathan offered to take her to RCW Steakhouse to celebrate. It was the first time he suggested taking her out in public. She'd understood he didn't want town gossips knowing their business, but it did sting a little that he didn't want to show her off.

Tonight was different, so she decided to treat herself to a new outfit at the Rancher's Daughter. Natalie didn't often visit the upscale fashion boutique owned by Chelsea's sister Morgan in the heart of downtown Royal, but a dinner out with Jonathan fit the occasion.

Morgan greeted her almost instantly upon her arrival with air kisses. "Natalie, it's so good to see you. Welcome to the Rancher's Daughter." Morgan was a vision in a green jumpsuit. It set off her long red hair and fair complexion perfectly.

Natalie smiled. "Thanks for the warm welcome." She glanced around and saw several other patrons milling about the store. "I've been dying to have a look around." She'd only been once with Chelsea for the grand opening.

"I have a slew of new items in the store. Walk around and have a look. Let me know if you need anything," Morgan replied. "I'm here to help."

"Definitely." Natalie walked over to the racks carrying several evening dresses. She was perusing the hangers when a pair of tawny brown legs came into her line of sight. She glanced up and saw a statuesque woman standing in front of her. She was taller than Natalie's five foot seven inches, slender with long dark brown hair and wearing what looked like designer clothes.

"Natalie Hastings?" the woman asked.

Natalie's brow crunched in confusion. "I'm sorry. Do we know each other?"

"No." The woman shook her head. "We've never met, but I have some insight on Jonathan Lattimore you might want to know."

Instantly, Natalie's radar went into high alert. When she glanced back at the woman, her eyes narrowed sharply and that's when recognition dawned. She was standing in front of *her*.

Anne Lattimore, Jonathan's ex-wife.

"Ah, so you realize who I am," Anne stated, folding her arms across her small breasts. Natalie hated that she felt inferior to Anne in her frumpy pantsuit. She'd come from a business meeting and hadn't thought about changing when she decided to pop into the store spur of the moment.

"I do, but I'm not sure what you and I would possibly have to discuss." Natalie sidestepped Anne to continue looking through the array of clothes Morgan had on display.

"Oh, I think we do," Anne stated, moving back into Natalie's path. "Especially when you tell the entire town you've got a thing for my husband."

Natalie turned to face her and her eyes flashed fire. "Ex-husband."

Anne shrugged. "Semantics."

"If you'll excuse me." Natalie kept searching the next rack, flinging back hanger after hanger. She wasn't even looking at the clothes anymore. She just wanted out, but she refused to make a scene. She glanced up and saw Morgan stepping forward to intervene, but Natalie shook her head. She could stand up to the likes of Anne. This woman hurt Jonathan and *she* was the reason he wasn't willing to commit or marry again. She wasn't interested in anything Anne had to say.

"I will *not* be excused," Anne said. "Because you're

wasting your time if you think Jonathan is some prize catch."

Natalie's head snapped up. "What are you talking about?"

"You think I can't tell you're sprung on him." Anne's voice rose several octaves and Natalie hated that several patrons were listening, or should she say eavesdropping, on their conversation. "The whole town can see it. You're not fooling anyone. But let me tell you something." She pointed her index finger in Natalie's face. "Jonathan is not husband material. If he can't commit to me—" she ran her fingers down her side "—he sure as hell won't commit to someone like you."

"You're really hateful, you know that?" Natalie had been faced with women like Anne her entire life and she refused to be put down again. "No wonder Jonathan didn't want to stay married to you."

"I divorced him!" Anne's face turned red. "Because he doesn't have it in him to commit to anyone. If I were you, I'd walk away now before he breaks your poor pathetic heart."

The dig hit the mark. Natalie wanted to recoil and hide away in a shell like a tortoise, but she refused to show Anne she'd hurt her, especially with everyone in the store openly staring at them. Instead, she lifted her chin and was about to give Anne a piece of her mind, but she didn't have to because Morgan intervened.

"Anne, I'm going to have to ask you to leave," Morgan said, moving between them.

"Why?" Anne huffed. "I didn't do anything

but tell her—" she inclined her head in Natalie's direction "—the truth."

"You're harassing my customers and I will not have it," Morgan added. "Leave. *Now.* And you're no longer welcome in my store."

"Fine." Anne tossed her hair back and hazarded a glance at Natalie. "But don't say I didn't warn you. Jonathan will never love you or anyone because he's never gotten over me." And with that stinging comment, Anne left the store.

"Ohmigod!" Morgan rushed over and touched Natalie's arm. "Are you okay? That woman has always been a bitch. I should've banned her years ago."

Natalie shook her head. She was far from okay. The things Anne said resonated because Natalie wondered them herself. Would Jonathan ever get over Anne and his divorce? Was Natalie spinning her wheels waiting for him to realize she was what he'd been looking for his whole life?

"You can't believe a thing that woman said. She was being spiteful and vindictive because she's jealous of you."

Natalie heard the words coming out of Morgan's mouth, but she was in too much of a daze. She felt like the walls were closing in and she couldn't breathe. All she could do was thank Morgan for the help and rush out of the store. Once outside, she leaned against the window and took in big gulps of air.

Was Anne telling the truth? She knew her "advice" was fueled by anger and jealousy, but her words made sense. She and Jonathan had been dating for two weeks and nothing had changed. Natalie thought she could accept loving him without the things she held dear like marriage and children, but she'd been wrong. She couldn't do this anymore. She had to face facts: she was in love with a man who refused to commit to her and was quite possibly still hung up on his ex-wife.

Sixteen

"Someone is pretty chipper," Jayden said when he stopped by Jonathan's office at the ranch to get him to sign some papers.

Jonathan grinned. "Yeah, I am." He was happy. If he was honest, it had been much too long since he'd felt this way. But ever since he'd begun seeing Natalie in Royal, he felt like his entire outlook on life had changed. She was a positive influence and he mostly never thought about all the bad stuff that happened to him. Instead, he focused on the good things, and Natalie was one of them.

It's why he'd finally decided they needed to go out for a real date. The last couple of weeks they'd been holed up at either his house or her cottage. Enough was enough; he needed to treat Natalie like the lady she was and not some random hookup he casually had sex with. He'd invited her to dinner tonight at the RCW Steakhouse. When dinner was over, he intended to take Natalie back to his place and make love to her until the sun rose.

"And is there a cause for such elation? Or shall I say who is the cause?" Jayden asked, sitting in the chair opposite Jonathan's desk.

Jonathan leaned back in his chair. "Yes, and you know who."

A wide smile curved Jayden's mouth. "I'm so glad to see you are letting someone in. Natalie is a spectacular lady. I can't wait to get to know her better."

Jonathan wasn't making any family introductions anytime soon. They were taking baby steps. The first being a dinner out on the town. "She is, and I'm taking her out to RCW tonight to show her how much I appreciate her."

"Grand gestures," Jayden said. "I approve. Though I wouldn't know about all that. I'm quite happy with my bachelorhood status."

Jonathan chuckled. "Enjoy, my friend, because you never know when Cupid's arrow is going to strike."

After Jayden left and Jonathan was closing up shop for the day, he received a call from Morgan Grandin. She didn't usually call him out of the blue. "Hey, Morgan, is everything okay?"

Morgan sighed. "I'm afraid not. An altercation took place at the Rancher's Daughter."

Jonathan sat upright in his chair. "Are you okay?"

Morgan let out a low laugh. "Nothing like that, but

I did want to make you aware that Anne made a visit to the store."

Now there was a name he didn't want to hear, especially not now when he was in a good headspace. "She did?"

"Yes. And it wasn't to buy clothes," Morgan replied. "She accosted Natalie at the store."

"What happened?" His voice was terse, but his body was already surging forward, ready for an attack.

"I couldn't hear the entire conversation. I only saw Anne getting in Natalie's face and the expression Natalie wore. Whatever Anne said, her words were upsetting."

"Thank you for letting me know. I'll take care of things from here."

"Of course," Morgan replied, "but if you don't mind my asking, why would Anne be getting into it with Natalie? Is something going on between you two?"

Although Jonathan was taking Natalie on a public date, he wasn't ready to reveal his love life to all his family and friends just yet. "I'll talk to you later, Morgan." He quickly ended the call before she could ask any more questions.

Steepling his fingers, Jonathan wondered what Anne and Natalie spoke about. What had she said that could have upset Natalie? He hoped Natalie wouldn't take anything his ex-wife said at face value, but there was only one way to find out. He had to talk to Natalie.

Natalie stared at her reflection in the mirror. As much as she wanted to get ready for her date with Jonathan, she couldn't. Outwardly, she looked fine, but inside she was a hot mess. Anne's angry words kept running through her mind like they were on some kind of interminable loop. All Natalie could hear was that Jonathan was never going to love her because he was still hung up on Anne.

That cut because no matter how often she told herself she could wait and see if Jonathan fell in love with her, deep down she knew better. She'd been holding out hope that the more time they spent together, he would rescind his no-marriage proclamation, but she was fooling herself.

When they came back to Royal, it had been easy to put those feelings on the shelf because Jonathan behaved like a total jerk by not reaching out to her. But then he recommended her company to Barbara and that's when Natalie realized she wasn't the only one infatuated. But was that all she was to him? A convenient sexual partner who was compatible in the bedroom?

She had to accept the reality of her situation and give up the dream that Jonathan would ever feel differently. Natalie couldn't regret the few weeks she'd spent with him. She lived out her fantasy. However, she told Jonathan she wanted the white picket fence, and she had to hold out until she got it.

The doorbell rang, interrupting her musings. When she glanced through the peephole, she saw it was Jonathan. He was early and she wasn't ready. She flung open the door.

"What are you doing here?" she asked. "I thought you said six thirty." It was only five thirty, but then looking at him, Natalie realized he wasn't dressed for dinner, either. Instead, he wore a serious expression. "Jonathan? Is everything okay?"

"I could ask you that," he said, stepping inside without waiting for an invitation.

"I don't follow."

He looked down at her and Natalie understood. He knew. Knew about Anne and what occurred at Morgan's store. "You heard?"

"Morgan called and told me my ex-wife accosted you. She said you were visibly shaken. What did she say to you, Natalie?"

Natalie spun away from him. "I don't want to talk about it, plus it doesn't matter anyway. I can't believe anything she says."

Jonathan touched her shoulder and spun her around to look at him. "Don't do that, Nat. Don't act as if you're not hurting. I can see that you are."

Darn. She thought she was doing a good job of not showing what was brewing inside. "I'm fine."

"Don't lie to me. I thought you said you would never do that."

He had her again. Natalie lowered her head. She thought about what edited version she could give Jonathan of what Anne told her, but she knew she couldn't do that because she deserved to hear what Jonathan had to say in response to Anne's words.

Natalie looked up into Jonathan's sincere brown eyes. "She accused me of being sprung on you, told me the whole town could see I was making a fool of myself over you, a man that wasn't husband material and would never commit to me."

"Natalie. I'm sorry. You have to know that she was lying," Jonathan stated.

"About which statement?"

"That you're making a fool out of yourself. You're not," Jonathan said. "You know how I feel about you."

Natalie's eyes narrowed. "Do I?"

He stepped backward as if he was flummoxed about why she would think otherwise. He never told her how he felt. "Yes, you do. Natalie. C'mon, don't let Anne get into your head."

"I'm not," Natalie responded. "After Anne confronted me, I realized that you would never commit because nothing has changed between us and that doesn't work for me, Jonathan. I want a commitment, marriage and babies, and if I stay with you, I would be settling for less than what I deserve and giving up my dreams for the future."

Jonathan huffed. "Why are you letting her do this? Anne said those things to hurt you. If I didn't want to be with you, I wouldn't be here."

"Anne didn't do anything but say what I already knew. You told me yourself that you would never marry. Has that changed?"

"We're getting off track. We've had an amazing couple of weeks together. In case you hadn't noticed, I can't seem to keep my hands off you."

He moved toward Natalie and tried to wrap his arms around her waist, but she pushed him away. She couldn't, *wouldn't* confuse the conversation by putting sex into the equation. She'd done that enough with Jonathan and right now she needed answers.

"Jonathan, stop it!" Natalie yelled.

"What?" he asked, moving away from her. "I'm trying to show you how much I enjoy being with you, Natalie."

"And that's the problem. Our relationship is physical, but I want more."

"I've been trying!" Jonathan exclaimed. "All our time isn't in the bedroom. We've done other activities."

"And afterward, we ended up having sex. And I can't do this anymore..." She was finding the courage to speak her truth. She had to be brave even though it hurt.

"You can't what? Believe in me?" Jonathan inquired. "Because I've never lied to you."

Tears slid down Natalie's cheeks because they were finally getting to the heart of the matter. Down to brass tacks and what she'd known but had tried to hide from. "I want a commitment, Jonathan. I deserve it. Can you give me that?"

"Natalie, don't do this," Jonathan pleaded.

"Call you out?" Natalie asked, raising her voice and wiping the tears on her cheeks with the back of her hand. For too long she had been covering up the truth because they shared a phenomenal physical connection, but no more.

"Just say it, Jonathan. Because right now, I need to hear it again. Maybe then it will finally sink in."

Jonathan stared back at Natalie's tearstained face. He hated seeing her crying and so upset and knowing he was the reason behind it. He wanted to be able to give her the commitment she deserved, but he wasn't able to.

It was unfair of him to take advantage of her infatuation with him and her inherent kindness and goodness any longer. He hadn't realized how much he needed some joy and happiness in his life until Natalie. She was like a breath of fresh air. But she was also a woman who wanted marriage and babies. He couldn't give her that, and the best thing he could do right now was set her free so she could find someone worthy of her— because he wasn't that man. He didn't deserve her.

"I'm sorry, Natalie," Jonathan said. "You'll never know how much, but I will never commit to you or anyone else."

Jonathan saw the moment his words reached her because a light went out in her eyes. He'd crushed her hopes and dreams. Natalie clutched her stomach as if she was going to be physically ill and bent over. Jonathan wanted to go to her. Hold her in his arms. Kiss her. Make love to her and tell her everything was going to be all right.

But it wasn't.

They couldn't continue like this because it wasn't what Natalie wanted and he would never want her to settle for less than what she deserved.

When she finally righted herself, she asked, "Because you'll never love anyone else because you've never gotten over Anne?"

The easiest thing to do would be to lie to Natalie saying he was still hung up on his ex-wife, but Jonathan was no coward. He had to be honest with her, even if it hurt.

"I'm not in love with Anne," Jonathan responded. "I'm not cut out for the long-term."

Natalie stood, nodding furiously and swiping away

tears off her cheeks. "You told me that. I should've listened."

"I wish I could be the man you need me to be."

This time when she looked at him, her eyes connected with his and they glittered with anger. "You can be, Jonathan, but you choose not to be. You've kept everything between us about sex so you can't be hurt. I'm here to tell you that people are going to let you down. That's life, but it doesn't make love and marriage wrong. You have to quit judging me and every other woman based on your past experience with Anne because she let you down. It's not fair to us and most of all, it's not fair to you."

"You don't understand." There was so much more to the story that he'd never shared with another soul. No one knew the heartache and pain he endured.

"And apparently I never will," Natalie said quietly. "I think it's best if you leave now."

Jonathan agreed. He picked up his Stetson and started toward the door, but then he couldn't resist going to Natalie one final time. He grasped her waist and at first, he thought she was going to resist, but she came to him like some limp rag doll.

He leaned and brushed his lips across her forehead and whispered, "You deserve the very best, Natalie Hastings. Thank you for sharing a few weeks with me. It's been the happiest I've been in a long time." Then he released her and walked out of her life.

Seventeen

"He didn't fight for me, Chelsea, for us, for what we could be," Natalie told her best friend later that evening when she sent out an emergency SOS. Chelsea left Nolan's and immediately rushed over to Natalie's cottage. "Instead, he gave me a forehead kiss and left. He left." Natalie snapped her fingers. "As if we meant nothing."

It's why she hadn't told him she loved him; she refused to give him those precious words knowing he didn't feel the same way, so she kept them to herself.

"I'm so sorry, Natalie," Chelsea said, consoling her. "I should never have advised you to chase after Jonathan. Not when I knew how strongly you felt about him."

"I don't blame you, Chelsea." Natalie sniffed into her Kleenex. "I blame Jonathan for being too cowardly to try again. So, what, Anne hurt him and did a number on him? No matter how many times you get on the horse and fall off, you're supposed to get back on. Instead, he's wallowing in his self-despair and carrying it around like some coat of armor."

Chelsea nodded. "I thought the more time you spent together, Jonathan would see what a great catch you are and that he didn't want to let you get away."

Natalie snorted. "He was more than willing to throw this fish back in the sea."

"Nat, I hope this doesn't deter you from trying again. You deserve a man who loves and wants you. Who's willing to fight for you."

"It won't deter me." Natalie shook her head. "If nothing else I think this experience taught me what I deserve and what I am and am not willing to accept. I think because it was Jonathan, I gave him way more latitude than I would any other man. Because for me, he's always been *the one*."

Chelsea nodded.

Natalie's head fell in her hands, and she began crying again in earnest. She couldn't stop herself. Once Jonathan walked out her door, she crumbled on the floor. It's where Chelsea found her after using the spare key—exactly where Jonathan left her.

"He broke my heart, Chelsea, and I let him. I didn't fight for what I wanted. All we were doing was hooking up."

"That's hogwash and you know it," Chelsea said. "You guys may have gotten busy quite a bit, but there was more to you than just a physical relationship. You told me so yourself."

"I was delusional. Like I was about everything where Jonathan was concerned."

"Hey." Chelsea lifted Natalie's chin. "I'm not going to let you get down on yourself. You misjudged him. We all make mistakes, but you were open and willing to give him your heart and if he can't see what a precious gift that is and grab it with both hands, he's a fool."

A smile formed on Natalie's lips. "Thank you, Chelsea. I don't know what I'd do without you."

Yeah, she did—she would drown herself in her despair by eating an entire peach pie.

Jonathan shrugged off his work jacket. He had been up with the sun because he needed physical labor to keep him busy and take his mind off Natalie and the look in her eyes when he once again confirmed he would never commit to her, love her like she wanted. He'd hurt her.

It had been two days since he left her Friday night and he was still reliving the moment, reliving the memories of their short time together. The way she laughed with him. The way she looked at him. The way she held him. When they were together, she felt so good, he never wanted to let her go. It made him want to become the man she needed him to be, but he couldn't. He couldn't take that risk. He was doing the right thing for both of them. She would get over him, over the possibility of them. She was better off without him and all his hang-ups.

"Whoa! What's with you this morning? You're attacking these chores like hay is your archenemy," Jayden said when he found Jonathan in the barn, hot and sweaty, helping the ranch hands with the horses and cleaning out stalls.

The devastation lurking in the brown depths of Natalie's eyes gutted Jonathan, and he'd been unable to sleep. "Couldn't sleep." Jonathan said, tossing a bale of hay across the stable, ignoring Jayden's attempt at humor.

"Oh Lord!" Jayden sighed audibly. "What the hell happened to make the old, sullen Jonathan return?"

"I'm not in the mood for your antics today, Jayden." Jonathan went to the next stall and began cleaning.

"I want to know how you can go from giddy happy one day to cold and mean the next."

Jonathan didn't want to listen to Jayden, so he grabbed his brother by the arm and pulled him toward his office down the hall. Once the door was closed, he pulled off his gloves one by one. "Natalie and I broke up."

Jayden frowned. "Why? What did you do?"

"Why do you assume I did something?" Jonathan said, plunking down in the executive chair behind his wood desk.

"Because Natalie is a great girl who adores you. The way she gushed about you at the TCC party was nothing short of romantic."

"Fine, then it was me. Natalie realized she was never going to change me into the commitment kind of man she wanted, the kind of man she deserved."

Jonathan was upset with himself for not expressing his feelings more clearly, so Natalie didn't see a ring on her finger. "It's for the best."

"What is?"

"That Natalie called things off. We were never going to work."

"That's a lie and you damn well know it," Jayden responded. "I haven't seen you this happy in, hell, I don't remember when. Natalie lit up your world and you're an idiot for letting a woman that fine get away."

"You're wrong."

"Wrong that you're afraid to admit you have feelings for Natalie? Oh no, I'm right about that. Don't tell me it won't burn you to see Natalie with another man."

Jonathan closed his eyes and thinking about Natalie with another man made his blood boil.

"What are you so afraid of, bro?" Jayden asked. "You have a good woman who is ready to devote her life to you and have a bunch of your babies. You should be snatching her up in a heartbeat because I promise you, your loss will be another's man gain."

Jayden's words remained with Jonathan long after he'd gone. He didn't know if he could change. The wounds Anne inflicted on his heart had scarred him. The past few weeks were the first time in nearly a decade he'd allowed himself to feel anything. And he had. He cared for Natalie a great deal.

No, it was more than that, but he refused to acknowledge those feelings. Instead, he pushed them down as far as they could go, because then he wouldn't have to put his heart on the line.

* * *

"Mrs. Lattimore, I'm so pleased to have you stop by," Natalie said when Jonathan's mother came to H & W Marketing's offices for an impromptu visit. The older woman was dressed in slacks, a silk shirt with a bow at the collar and pumps.

"I thought it was high time I meet your business partner, Brent. Is he here?" Barbara inquired.

Natalie was having a hard time believing Jonathan's mother was in her office because it made her think about Jonathan, and she'd tried her best to push him to the back of her mind. It was hard because time stagnated and after Chelsea left, the weekend dragged on. Natalie had paced, unable to sleep. She missed him. *Loved him.*

She was glad when Monday came. It hadn't taken much effort to get out of her pajamas she'd stayed in over the entire weekend. Now she could focus on work rather than how she'd foolishly allowed herself to get caught up in a sexual affair with a man afraid of commitment.

"Uh…no, I'm sorry. Brent is at a meeting," Natalie responded. "If we had known you were coming in, we would have made sure he was here."

"Oh, it's nothing." Barbara patted Natalie's hand. "It was spur of the moment." She glanced around the open office.

"Can I get you anything?" Natalie asked. "Coffee, tea, juice?"

"Coffee would be lovely, thank you."

"Coming right up." Natalie walked to the kitchen

and was busying herself with the Keurig machine and selecting one of the delicious brews when she turned and found Barbara in the doorway staring at her.

"Why did you break up with my son?" Barbara inquired.

Natalie dropped the Keurig pod in her hand. "Ma'am?"

Barbara laughed and picked the pod up off the floor and handed it to Natalie. "Did you think I didn't figure out you and my son had become—" she paused as if searching for the right word "—better acquainted since Galveston?"

"Uh, no," Natalie said. "I hadn't realized."

"Well, I did. And since then, I've noticed how taken my son is with you. I see how he looks at you when no one is watching."

"I'm sorry, you're quite mistaken."

"Oh, I didn't say he knew it yet," Barbara replied with a wide smile, "but he will. Give him time."

"I'm sorry, Barbara, but I'm afraid I can't talk about Jonathan with you. I hope he's not the reason you gave me your business."

Barbara laughed. "My darling, I don't make business decisions based on who my son is sleeping with."

Natalie blushed furiously and lowered her head.

"Please don't be embarrassed. I only meant that I hired you based on your skill set and what you and your company bring to the table. I like having a local firm I can come to."

"I'm so pleased."

Barbara nodded. "Good." She stepped toward Natalie and lightly placed her hand on her shoulder. "Anne was not the right fit for Jonathan. I knew that from the start, but you have to let young people make their own mistakes. I'm asking that you keep an open mind where Jonathan is concerned. I heard how much you care for him on that live audio. It's why I sent him to Galveston. And I've seen how being with you the last month has changed him."

When Natalie tried to interrupt her, Barbara shook her head. "Don't try to deny it. I know you've been seeing each other since Galveston and I've been so happy, but last night when I saw my son, he'd reverted to the sullen man he was before he left. I can only imagine he's pushed you away somehow because that's what Lattimore men do, but he'll come around."

"You don't know that."

Barbara smiled. "I know my son. Promise me that you will give him the chance to redeem himself, because I believe he cares more for you than he's willing to admit."

"He has to want to change and right now, Barbara, I don't think he's capable."

"Don't underestimate him, Natalie. He might surprise you." Barbara glanced at the Cartier watch on her wrist. "Oh my, look at the time, I have to get going for another appointment. Please give Brent my apologies and let him know I'd like for the three of us to have lunch day after tomorrow at the ranch, my treat."

"We would love that," Natalie replied. "Thank you so much."

Once Jonathan's mother had gone, Natalie wondered what her visit was about. Barbara always seemed to be one step ahead of them and knew details about their relationship. They had kept their relationship a secret, staying at each other's respective homes. Then again, Royal was a small town; maybe they slipped up at some point and someone saw them?

Natalie doubted it mattered. What was done was done. It would be foolish of her to get her hopes up and think Jonathan was suddenly about to confess his love just because his mother thought he would realize his mistake. He had plenty of chances to tell her how he felt. Instead, he repeatedly told her didn't want love or marriage. She had to accept his decision and move on with her life. Surely there was another man who could rock her world like Jonathan.

Natalie sighed. She doubted it. Jonathan would always be her vacation crush.

Eighteen

Jonathan thought long and hard about Jayden's advice and analyzed his feelings about Natalie. He'd never met a woman so kind, loving and giving. She opened her heart to him from the start even though he didn't deserve it. She gave herself over and over again and all he did was take and take and never offer her anything in return.

But did she leave him?

No.

Night after night she came to him and showed him with her actions and with her body how much she cared for him. And dare he hope, loved him? He hoped so, because he missed her.

He was in love with Natalie. With her mind. With her spirt. And with her body.

He wanted to shout it from the rooftops, but then

he remembered the pain on her beautiful face and the way she'd crumpled when he'd told her he would never commit to her, never love her. He thought he was being cruel to be kind. Instead, he'd hurt the one person in the world who loved him more than his own family. He would never forgive himself for the way he ended things between them. He needed to make amends by telling Natalie what happened between him and Anne. He would tell her how much he loved her and pray that she might someday give him another chance to make things right.

Natalie was feeling uneasy when she and Brent returned to the Lattimore ranch for lunch two days later. She was fearful of running into Jonathan. What would she say? This would be even worse than when they returned from Galveston and were awkward around each other.

"Are you sure you're okay with this?" Brent asked as they drove. "If you want, we can cancel."

She had finally broken down and told Brent everything about her and Jonathan's nearly monthlong affair. He'd been surprised but understood their need for privacy. Brent wasn't, however, happy with Jonathan. He thought that Jonathan's refusal to commit to a relationship with Natalie was a cop-out.

"Cancel lunch with one of our biggest clients?" Natalie asked, glancing out the window. "No way." Their business was at stake, and she wouldn't do anything to jeopardize it, even if it meant her heart was broken at seeing the eldest son.

Thankfully, when they arrived, she didn't see his truck and Natalie found that she, Brent and Barbara could settle in for an easy lunch. Mrs. Lattimore had gone to a lot of trouble and prepared a three-course lunch.

From the mushroom and truffle soufflé with crispy shiitakes to the red snapper with root vegetables, every bite was sinfully delicious.

"You really didn't have to make lunch, Barbara," Natalie said, wiping her mouth with a napkin.

"I want you to know and appreciate the brand you're representing," Barbara responded.

Brent patted his full stomach. "We certainly do."

"When one of my readers picks up that pot or pan with my label to make a dish for their family, I want them to know everything was thought out."

"How did you get into cooking?" Natalie asked. Her grandmother was an excellent cook and she helped Natalie master a few dishes, so she was proficient in the kitchen, but she was by no means a chef.

"When I started cooking for my husband, my mother-in-law wasn't a fan. She thought my husband would go hungry. Much to my chagrin, she took me under her wing. I learned what I could and then added my own touch to each dish. The rest, as they say, is history."

"I love that story. It's authentic and will go well with selling your products," Natalie stated, sipping on the Arnold Palmer that Barbara had remembered she liked.

"It's important to me that I'm one hundred percent myself in everything I represent. The companies we choose to partner with for my products must understand that."

"We'll make sure of it," Brent stated.

"How about some dessert?" Barbara suggested. "I have an heirloom apple tart puff pastry with goat cheese ice cream waiting for you."

Natalie had a weakness for sweet things. "I would love some, thank you."

"Coming right up," Barbara said, "Brent, would you like to join me?"

Brent raised a brow and glanced at Natalie. She didn't know what Jonathan's mother had up her sleeve, but she nodded. Brent and Barbara departed the dining room several minutes later. Natalie was writing a few notes on her notepad when she noticed she wasn't alone in the room.

Jonathan.

She sucked in a breath. What was he doing here? Barbara must have set this up. Natalie rose to her feet. "I can't do this with you, Jonathan. Not now. I'm here on business." And her heart couldn't take another beating and keep ticking.

"Can you spare a few minutes? I really need to talk to you."

Natalie glanced away and then back at Jonathan. His eyes looked tired and his face drawn. It looked like he hadn't slept much, same as her. Each night when she reached for him, she found a cold sheet. "All right." She sat down and rather than sit beside her, Jonathan sat across from her at the table.

"I want to tell you about my marriage to Anne," Jonathan started.

Natalie leaned backward. She wasn't ready for that

bombshell. Every time she asked Jonathan to open up about his past, about his marriage, he clammed up. Now in the final hour, he wanted to talk. "You don't have to do that."

"Yes, I do, because that's the only way you're going to understand my perspective."

She sighed. She supposed hearing his reasoning might give Natalie the closure she needed to move on. "Okay. Go ahead."

"Anne and I got married young," Jonathan said. "Neither of our parents supported the marriage, but we were determined to do it anyway and went to a justice of the peace. I was just getting started at the ranch and determined to prove to my father and my grandfather I had the chops to manage the ranch someday. They were doubtful, given my decision-making with such a hasty marriage."

"What happened?"

"Anne got jealous of the time I was spending at work and learning the family business. She got more and more clingy and complained nonstop that I was never there for her and wouldn't be for any kids we planned on. I told her I wasn't ready to start a family for a few years. Then she discovered she was pregnant. She terminated it."

"Ohmigod!" Natalie covered her mouth with her hand. "Had you discussed the termination?"

Jonathan shook his head. "No. I didn't even know she was pregnant, and I don't think she ever planned on telling me, but during one nasty fight she told me what she'd done. I was devastated. I blamed myself. I wasn't there for her. I made her feel like she had to take such a drastic action without speaking to me first. And Anne, well, she blamed me, too. Told me I had never really committed to her and if I couldn't do that, how could I be a father? She said I was more concerned with the ranch than our marriage and she wanted a divorce."

"After such a horrible experience I can see why you never wanted to get married again. You lost trust in your spouse."

"And in myself, Natalie. I've been haunted by the loss of that child, and I got it in my head that I was being punished and I didn't deserve happiness."

"Jonathan, that's not true. Anne made the choice to terminate the pregnancy, not you. You have to stop blaming yourself."

"I don't know how, Natalie. I've carried this load for so long. I never thought I deserved happiness until I found it with you. My brother saw it. Said he'd never seen me as happy as I've been in the last month. And that's all because of you."

Natalie smiled. "I appreciate you saying that." She ached for him and for the pain he was going through, but she'd given him her whole heart. She practically gift-wrapped it and he'd trounced on it. She wasn't sure she could go back down that road again. She needed to accept that Jonathan's heart might be damaged beyond repair. "But I can't be with someone who clings to past pain or who throws me away when they're hurting. I know I may not seem special, but..."

"Stop that, Natalie!" Jonathan's expression was thunderous, and he slammed his fist on the table. "You *are* special. You're special to me. Please believe that you've made me happier than I've been in a long time, and I don't want to lose that. I want to bask in that happiness."

A tear leaked out from her eyes. "You told me you didn't want to be with me. Could never love me."

"Natalie." He closed his eyes and when he opened them again, she could see tears on his lashes. "I said that because I was afraid. I was pushing you away before you could hurt me because I was afraid to take a risk. But deep down, I knew that you never could. I was dead and cold inside until you came along and brought me back to life. You've reminded me what true love looks like."

"You can't say these things, Jonathan. Because quite honestly, I don't know if I can believe them." She lowered her head and tried to take a deep breath, but her heart was constricting.

"Can you believe that I love you?" Jonathan inquired. "Because I do. I love you, Natalie Hastings. I think I knew it after we were together in Galveston, but I pushed the feelings down. I acted like they didn't exist, but I don't want to do that anymore. I want to embrace life and all that it has to offer *with you* because missing you has made me realize I can't live without you. Please tell me I haven't destroyed the feelings you had for me?"

Natalie swallowed. When she saw him in the doorway her defenses had instantly gone up but hearing Jonathan's declaration of love was more than she could have ever hoped for. It made her want to be honest and more open than she'd ever been.

"My love for you isn't that fragile, Jonathan. It doesn't come and go like a hot Texas breeze. I was hurt and angered by the words you said, but it doesn't change anything. I love you, too."

"You do?"

"C'mon," Natalie said, smiling across the table at him. "I told the entire town and anyone listening on Facebook Live that you were the most amazing man I'd ever met and that hasn't changed. And now that I've gotten to know you, it's even more true."

"Can you forgive me for being such an insensitive and unfeeling jerk?" Jonathan asked.

Natalie wanted to believe love was enough, but she also knew that one thing could end this reconciliation. Right here and right now. "Of course I can, but what about children? Do you want them?"

Jonathan understood Natalie's reticence. He'd just told her that he was haunted by the loss of a child. A child he'd mourned for over eight years, but he was over grieving a little soul that wasn't meant to be. "I do want children, Natalie. I want them with you."

"Are you sure?"

Jonathan hated that she still had doubts, so he nearly topped his chair as he rushed to her. He squatted and faced her, cupping her cheeks. "Listen to me, I know you may not want to believe me when I tell you this, but I do want children. I can see now that the reason I didn't want kids with Anne was because early on I realized my mistake and that our marriage wasn't going to work out. But I'm done moping about the past. I want a future with you, Natalie. These last several days have proven to me that I can't live without you, and I don't even want to try."

"You can't?"

"There is no one else for me but you, Natalie." A tear slid down Jonathan's cheek. "I've even had visions of starting a family with you. We'd have the most beautiful babies with your round face and your big brown eyes." He grasped both her hands. "Please give me another chance." He kissed her hands. "I know I don't deserve you, but I promise you I will spend the rest of my life winning back your trust as long as you love me."

His heart was bursting open with love and when Natalie's eyes filled with tears, Jonathan thought it might be over, but then she threw herself against him and he hugged her tightly to his chest.

His heart thundered like the beat of a thousand African drums until she said, "I love you, Jonathan, so much. You mean everything to me. And I'm yours, body and soul."

He closed his eyes and cradled Natalie close. "I can't tell you how afraid I was that I'd lost you. I gave you every reason to turn your back on me."

Natalie looked up at him, her eyes overflowing with tears again, and Jonathan knew he'd found the woman he was meant to spend the rest of his days with. "What do you say we get out of here?" He rose to his feet and began leading her toward the door.

"I can't leave," Natalie said. "What about your mother?" She glanced at the door.

"My mother was in on it the entire time. You know

she loves matchmaking." Jonathan smiled. "I asked her to invite you here because I didn't think you would see me."

"You mischievous…" She didn't get another word out because Jonathan was covering her lips in a kiss that sent brilliant fireworks exploding through his chest. A kiss that felt right.

When they finally parted, Natalie said, "Take me home."

He tightened her in his embrace. "With pleasure." Lifting her in his arms, he carried her out the door and toward their forever future.

Nineteen

"You look amazing, babe," Jonathan said, taking her hand and walking her into the Texas Cattleman's Club a few days later. Natalie had opted to a wear a draped black halter maxi dress that tied at her neck. It was the perfect figure-flattering maxi for a summer evening. They matched because Jonathan filled out his black suit with a silver tie quite nicely.

Summer was officially over, and the club was embracing the end of season by having a party on the club grounds. They'd both completely forgotten because they'd been wrapped up in each other's arms after days apart. It was Barbara who sent a subtle reminder text to Jonathan's phone that their appearance was required.

As they made their way to the rear terrace, Natalie thought the club would have gone for a good old-fashioned barbecue, but instead a tropical theme was on display complete with string lights, freshly picked colorful flowers, tropical linens and gold-plated cutlery. There was even a champagne bar for guests to choose their favorite juice to go with the beverage. What caught Natalie's attention was the large video screen showing music videos from the summer's biggest hits. Lucky for her, she had no intention of being part of the festivities after the last debacle. She wanted to keep a low profile.

"Look who's finally here." Barbara smiled broadly when they approached. She rushed forward to greet Natalie. "I'm so happy the two of you worked things out."

"Oh, I think we had a little push," Natalie said with a wink. She'd had no idea his mother *and* Brent had been in on the action using H & W Marketing business to get Natalie to the Lattimore ranch, but it worked, and Natalie couldn't be happier. She and Jonathan were talking about their future and what that looked like.

When she confessed her feelings for Jonathan over the jumbotron, she never imagined they would end up like this. Sure, she hoped, but the reality far surpassed her wildest dreams. Jonathan was everything she could ever want, and Natalie couldn't wait for the day when she would become his wife. It was early days yet, but she knew in her heart of hearts that he was the man for her.

Just then, Vic Grandin and Aubrey Collins walked into the crowd. They were holding hands and getting open-mouthed stares and curious glances at their appearance. The couple used to date but had an acrimonious split years ago. It was shocking to see the two of them together.

"Did you know about this?" Jonathan inquired, glancing down at Natalie.

"Not at all." Natalie shook her head. "Chelsea never said a word. After Aubrey fell off the podium at the last Cattleman's Club party and hit her head, I'd heard she had amnesia, but not much else since."

"They used to date back in the day," Jonathan replied. "Once upon a time they were inseparable. Vic used to bring Aubrey to all our family events."

"Well, from the looks of it, they might be back together."

"I hope so," Jonathan replied. "They were very much in love, kind of like how we are right now." He bent his head to brush his lips softly across hers.

Natalie loved that Jonathan was willing to show PDA, especially because this was their first official outing as a couple. Like Vic and Aubrey, they were getting their share of looks and whispers in the crowd, but Natalie took it all in stride, because this time she had her man. "Then let's hope they found their way back to each other."

He kissed her again and the kiss might have gotten more passionate if Chelsea and Nolan hadn't strolled over and coughed very loudly. They pulled apart quickly and Natalie knew she had to have a guilty look on her face at having been caught making out. She hadn't had the chance to tell Chelsea she and Jonathan were officially a couple because they hadn't been able to get enough of each other the last few days and stayed holed up at his house making up for lost time.

Chelsea smiled knowingly. Her long brown hair flowed in gentle waves down her back, and she wore a strapless maxi dress with palm leaves all over it. Chelsea leaned in for a hug. "Jonathan. I'm so glad to see you came to your senses and didn't let this one—" she inclined her head to Natalie at his side "—get away."

"Yes, I did, and I'm a lucky man," Jonathan responded.

"And don't you forget it." Chelsea pointed her index finger at him. "Natalie is one in a million."

Jonathan looked down at her and said, "Yes, she is. Natalie, will you excuse me for a moment?"

"Of course," Natalie and Chelsea said in unison.

"Nolan, could you assist me for a moment? I need help with something," Jonathan said.

"Sure thing." Nolan gave Chelsea a shrug when she gave him a questioning look. Then the two men quickly disappeared through the crowd.

"I wonder what he's up to?" Chelsea asked, inclining her head in the direction the men had gone.

Natalie shrugged. "Doesn't matter to me." She grinned broadly. She was on cloud nine.

"I love seeing that silly grin on your face," Chelsea said. "Last weekend you were heartbroken, so to see you like this…well, it's exactly what I wished for you. To find the love I've found with Nolan."

"Thank you, Chelsea."

Suddenly, Jonathan's face popped up on the enormous video screen behind Chelsea. "What in the world!" Natalie gasped.

"My name is Jonathan Lattimore and I'm here to-night to tell you all about the love of my life. You might remember her, Natalie Hastings. She announced her feelings for me at the last TCC party and I thought it fitting that I should return the favor and tell you how much I adore her. She's smart and funny, kind and giving, open and honest. She's a good woman. And that's why I'm asking her, here, in front of all of you, if she will do me the honor of making me the happiest man alive."

To Natalie's utter shock, the video caption read "Will You Marry Me?"

"Ohmigod!" Natalie clasped her hand over her mouth. She turned around to look for Jonathan in the crowd, but she didn't have to look far because Chelsea had gone, and Jonathan was right behind her on one knee holding an enormous diamond ring in a velvet box.

"I'll ask you again, Natalie Marie Hastings," Jonathan said. "Will you marry me?"

"Yes, yes, a hundred times, yes."

There was applause and cheers as Natalie flung herself into his arms and Jonathan caught her as she knew he always would. Then he brought his lips to hers in the sweetest, most tender kiss imaginable before slipping the ring on her finger.

Suddenly, all of their friends and family were gathered around them, congratulating them on their engagement. There were hugs and tears of joy from Chelsea and Barbara, who gushed about her matchmaking skills. Heck, even Jonathan's brother, Jayden, welcomed her into the family.

"I always knew you two would seal the deal." Jayden

winked and then he was off to chat with one of his many female admirers.

"Natalie Hastings, have you been keeping Jonathan a secret from us?" her grandmother asked, coming toward them with her hands on her hips. Obviously Ben and Barbara had invited them. This made the proposal even more perfect.

It was Jonathan who answered. "I'm sorry, Mr. and Mrs. Hastings, it was all on me. Natalie wanted to tell you, but I kept our relationship hush-hush. Well...until now."

"As long as our daughter is happy," her grandfather said, looking at Natalie's beaming face, "that's all that matters to us."

"I'm very happy," Natalie responded, and leaned over to give them both a hug and a kiss.

"Welcome to the family, Jonathan." Her grandfather shook Jonathan's hand.

Once all the congratulations were over, Natalie and Jonathan wanted to celebrate alone and in private. They were so eager, they couldn't wait to get home and poked their heads into one of the club's pool cabanas. Finding it empty, they locked the doors, sealing them in and everyone else out.

Their eyes met and Jonathan's gaze was hot and dark. Natalie welcomed it. They reached for each other in a hungry, demanding kiss. Their tongues stroked and intertwined together, causing Natalie's entire body to go up in flames. She savagely began yanking at the buttons on Jonathan's shirt and they went flying.

She wanted him. *Now.*

Jonathan must have felt the same way because he relieved Natalie of her dress in two seconds flat. Then he was kissing her again, stroking the curve of her waist before coming to her panties. Gently, he pulled them off until he was kneeling in front of her.

"I want to worship you with my mouth," Jonathan said, and then his tongue was between her legs. He pushed her thighs apart and spread her wide. Natalie clutched at his shoulders to stay upright as he greedily tasted his fill. She cried out when the first rush of her orgasm took over her, and when her legs could no longer support her, they fell to the floor in a mass of limbs.

Jonathan shifted away from her long enough to remove the rest of his clothing and don a condom. Then he was right back where she wanted, angling her hips and pushing all the way to the hilt with one powerful thrust.

"Jonathan," Natalie moaned, wrapping her legs around him and pressing closer. She needed to feel his strength, feel his love. Jonathan gave her exactly what she needed. He grabbed her hips and slowly began pumping in and out in a delicious rhythm. The passion was so intense, the emotion so thick, they were both carried away. It was the most beautiful culmination of their love for each other.

And when their mouths fused once more, they kissed with abandon and totally forgot the world outside the cabana doors because the love inside with each other was all that mattered.

* * * * *

Don't miss the next installment in the
Texas Cattleman's Club: Ranchers and Rivals series

An Ex to Remember
by Jessica Lemmon

#2899 BEST MAN RANCHER
The Carsons of Lone Rock • by Maisey Yates
Widow Shelby Sohappy isn't looking for romance, but there's something enticing about rancher Kit Carson, especially now that they're thrown together for their siblings' wedding. As one night together turns into two, can they let go of their past to embrace a future?

#2900 AN EX TO REMEMBER
Texas Cattleman's Club: Ranchers and Rivals
by Jessica Lemmon
After a fall, Aubrey Collins wakes up with amnesia—and believing her ex, rancher Vic Grandin, is her current boyfriend! The best way to help her? Play along! But when the truth comes to light, their second chance may fall apart...

#2901 HOW TO MARRY A BAD BOY
Dynasties: Tech Tycoons • by Shannon McKenna
To help launch her start-up, Eve Seaton accepts an unbelievable offer from playboy CTO Marcus Moss: his connections for her hand in marriage, which will let him keep his family company. But is this deal too good to be true?

#2902 THE COMEBACK HEIR
by Janice Maynard
Home due to tragedy, exes Felicity Vance and Wynn Oliver don't expect to see one another, but Wynn needs a caregiver for the baby niece now entrusted in his care. But when one hot night changes everything, will secrets from their past ruin it all?

#2903 THE PREGNANCY PROPOSAL
Cress Brothers • by Niobia Bryant
Career-driven Montgomery Morgan and partying playboy chef Sean Cress have one fun night together, no-strings...until they discover she's pregnant. Ever the businesswoman, she proposes a marriage deal to keep up appearances. But no amount of paperwork can hide the undeniable passion between them!

#2904 LAST CHANCE REUNION
Nights at the Mahal • by Sophia Singh Sasson
The investor who fashion designer Nisha Chawla is meeting is...her ex, Sameer Singh. He was her first love before everything went wrong, and now he's representing his family's interests. As things heat up, she must hold on to her heart *and* her business...

YOU CAN FIND MORE INFORMATION ON UPCOMING HARLEQUIN TITLES, FREE EXCERPTS AND MORE AT HARLEQUIN.COM.

HDCNM0822

*Recording studio exec Miles Woodson needs a
showstopping act for his charity talent show,
and R&B superstar Cambria Harding fits the bill.
But when long days working together become steamy
nights, can these opposites make both their passion
project and relationship work?*

Read on for a sneak peek at
What Happens After Hours
by Kianna Alexander

"There's no need to insult me, Cambria. After all, we'll
be seeing a lot of each other over the next two weeks."

"Oh, I see. You're the type that can dish it, but can't
take it. Ain't that something?" she scoffed, then shook her
head. "Let's make a deal—I'll show you the same level
of respect you show me." She grabbed her handbag from
the table. "So remember the next time you open your
mouth, you can expect me to match whatever energy you
throw out."

He watched her, silently surveying the way her glossy lips pursed into a straight line, the defiant tilt of her chin, the challenge in her eyes. She was mesmerizing, disconcerting even. No woman had ever affected him this way before. *She knocks me so off balance, but for some reason, I like it.*

Her lips parted. "Why are you staring at me like that?"

Love Harlequin romance?

DISCOVER.

Be the first to find out about promotions, news and exclusive content!

Facebook.com/HarlequinBooks

Twitter.com/HarlequinBooks

Instagram.com/HarlequinBooks

Pinterest.com/HarlequinBooks

YouTube.com/HarlequinBooks

ReaderService.com

EXPLORE.

Sign up for the Harlequin e-newsletter and download a free book from any series at **TryHarlequin.com**

CONNECT.

Join our Harlequin community to share your thoughts and connect with other romance readers!
Facebook.com/groups/HarlequinConnection